Prescription: Romance™

A tug at the hem of his T-shirt caught his attention.

He glanced down at the little girl clutching a stuffed animal in one hand. A knot formed in his chest as his memories formed a bittersweet picture of his own daughter at this age. Tanya had always grabbed his pant leg to get his attention.

Carlie stared into Ben's face. "It's Mother's Day and we're having a picnic. Want to eat with us?"

While Kelly waited with bated breath for his reply, the harsh lines around his mouth softened. "Maybe next time."

Jessica Matthews's interest in medicine began at a young age and she nourished it with medical stories and hospital-based television programs. After a stint as a teenage candy-striper, she pursued a career as a clinical laboratory scientist. When not writing, or on duty, she fills her day with countless family- and school-related activities. Jessica lives in the central United States with her husband, daughter and son.

Prescription: Romance™

A HERO FOR MOMMY
JESSICA MATTHEWS

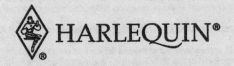

HARLEQUIN®

TORONTO • NEW YORK • LONDON
AMSTERDAM • PARIS • SYDNEY • HAMBURG
STOCKHOLM • ATHENS • TOKYO • MILAN • MADRID
PRAGUE • WARSAW • BUDAPEST • AUCKLAND

To lab personnel everywhere

ACKNOWLEDGMENTS

My special thanks go to Chris Stewart at the
Sundance Chamber of Commerce for patiently answering
my questions about the community, and to both Trudi and Susan
at the Crook County Memorial Hospital
for their generosity in sharing information
so I'd have a model for my fictional hospital.
Any errors are my own.

ISBN 0-373-63122-7

A HERO FOR MOMMY

First North American Publication 1999.

Visit us at www.romance.net

Printed in U.S.A.

PROLOGUE

'I NEED a favor, Ben.'

Hunched over his pool cue, ready to take his shot, Benjamin Shepard cast his younger brother a benevolent smile, before sending the seven ball into the side pocket. He'd lost count of the number of 'favors' that he'd performed over the years at Tom's request.

He eyed his next move as he skirted the Dalmatian, lying on the floor near the billiard table. 'What is it this time?'

Tom appeared affronted. His blue eyes turned a darker hue as did his fair complexion. 'What do you mean, "this time"? I haven't asked for anything since—'

'Your last visit,' Ben answered, tapping the white ball. It kissed the six ball, sending it on a gentle roll into a nearby pocket. 'Which, I might add, was a month ago. Of course, that's not mentioning the huge favor you called about the other night.' He raised one eyebrow as he sidestepped the table again. 'Holding our rental house vacant, if I'm not mistaken.'

Tom clutched his cue. 'Did you?'

'Did I what?' Ben noticed Tom's white-knuckled grip before he sent another ball scurrying into its pocket. Whatever was on Tom's mind must be important.

Tom rolled his eyes, clearly as exasperated by his older brother's deliberately obtuse demeanor as by his skill. 'Keep the house vacant.'

'At the moment I haven't accepted any contracts,' Ben prevaricated, 'although the real estate agent has someone

5

interested so unless you can give me a good reason—
and I do mean a *good* one—for refusing his offer…'

Tom's pose relaxed, the worry lines on his boyish face
erased by Ben's news. 'I've already given out the key.'

Ben halted his survey of the table to study his sibling
through narrowed eyes. 'You've already given out the
key,' he echoed.

Tom nodded. 'Sure did.'

Momentarily at a loss for words, Ben refocused his
attention on the game. While part of his mind planned
his next shot the other part contemplated Tom's news.
Knowing his brother's weakness for so-called strays and
their stories of woe, he could imagine the scenario about
to unfold. He heaved a heartfelt sigh. 'I'm listening.'

'I met a woman in Sheridan,' Tom began.

Unable to stop himself, Ben grimaced.

'Hey, don't look at me like that,' Tom protested. 'It
isn't what you think.'

Aiming for one of his solids, Ben hit the white ball
again. It veered slightly and struck one of Tom's stripes
instead. He frowned as he straightened. 'How do you
know what I'm thinking?'

Tom glared. 'I just do. If I've seen that look on your
face once I've seen it a hundred times. You've already
decided that you won't like what I'm going to tell you.'

With a great deal of effort, since Tom had accurately
described Ben's thoughts, Ben settled his face into the
professional mask that he normally reserved for his patients. 'Sorry. Go ahead.'

Tom's eyes narrowed. 'You'll keep an open mind?'

'I'll try.' Knowing some of the scrapes Tom had got
into over the years, he couldn't promise more than that.

'I met this woman,' Tom began again. 'Kelly Evers.'
He paused, studying Ben's face for a reaction.

Ben raised an eyebrow. 'And?'

Apparently reassured by his brother's restraint, Tom continued. 'After you told me about Ed Townsend's cancer, and how he was desperate for someone to fill in for him at the lab while he's undergoing chemotherapy, I called Don Jamison in Human Resources and recommended Kelly. She's a lab tech and works for a temporary help agency. Knowing she didn't have another job lined up, it was the least I could do.'

'I'm sure,' Ben replied dryly. 'I presume you gave her the key.'

Tom grinned as he took his turn at the table. 'You bet. Don't worry, you're going to love her. She's bright and witty and charming and so talented. And can she cook! She makes the most fantastic meals out of nothing. What she can do with a can of tuna....' He smacked his lips, before sending balls ricocheting off the sides.

'I'll bet.' Ben's sarcasm went unnoticed. Tom was too busy watching a striped ball roll into the far left pocket. Purely by chance, Ben decided. Tom didn't play with any particular strategy in mind.

'She dotes on Carlie—'

'Who's Carlie?'

'Her daughter. She'll turn five in a few weeks. Anyway, Kelly knows how to pinch pennies, but you wouldn't know it by looking at her. She's one classy lady.'

Ben's mental radar screamed an alert and, involuntarily, his grip on the cue tightened. A young woman—a single mother—with her hundred and one ways to prepare tuna, would no doubt love to latch her greedy claws onto an up-and-coming anesthesiologist. What woman in her right mind wouldn't dream of trading her shoe-string-budget cookbook and can opener for filet mignon recipes and steak sauce?

'She's thirty,' Tom continued, blissfully unaware of

Ben's frozen alertness as he sent more balls careening around the table. Two dropped into their holes. 'And I think I'm—'

'Hold on a minute,' Ben interrupted, holding his hands—including the one clutching the cue—in the air in the classic 'stop' gesture. He didn't want to hear the dreaded phrase 'in love' again, and he mentally wagered that those were the words he was about to hear. 'You're twenty-seven. I didn't know you were interested in an older woman, much less one with a ready-made family.'

'Kelly is special,' Tom insisted, 'and that's why I'm asking you for this favor. I want you to help her settle in, both at the hospital and around town. I'd do it but it's impossible for me as I'm so far away.'

'I don't have time to nursemaid your girlfriend,' Ben said sharply. 'I'm up to my eyeballs in hospital budgets, fiscal studies and my own patients.'

'Just check on her once in a while. Make her feel welcome. Take her under your wing, so to speak. That's all. No big deal.' This time he'd only rearranged the balls on the table and he shook his head with minor disgust.

Ben rubbed his face. Tom's idea of 'no big deal' didn't match his. As a child, Tom would bring home neglected animals because he couldn't bear to see them mistreated. Inevitably Ben would inherit the responsibility of their care while Tom blithely rescued something else. The Dalmatian at his feet—Percy—had been a case in point. However, Tom's generosity hadn't stopped with animals.

Tom would volunteer him to act as chaperon at his high school dances whenever Ben planned a weekend visit. During the course of those evenings Tom would introduce him to a shy wallflower and expect him to give her a night, or at least a few dances, to remember.

Ben had finally put his foot down and threatened bodily harm after Tom had partnered him with a young lady who'd possessed the personality of a rock. He'd undergo the worst medical procedure known to man rather than experience a similar situation again.

Seeing a distinct parallel between then and now, Ben opened his mouth to refuse.

'Just show her that Sundance, Wyoming, is a great place to live,' Tom coaxed.

The game forgotten, Ben reminded him, 'I'm not on the town's welcoming committee. Besides, she's only going to be here a short time.'

'Maybe. Maybe not. Don mentioned the possibility of adding a permanent lab position because of the increased workload your satellite clinics have generated. Kelly may like Sundance so well she'll apply for the job. At any rate, you owe me.'

Ben stared at his fair-haired brother in disbelief. 'I owe *you*?'

Tom nodded. 'Remember when Justin lined you up with his cousin for a blind date a few months ago? I took your place.'

'Oh, yeah.' Ben remembered meeting the young woman at the clinic. She'd walked through the exam rooms, wearing some wild-looking caftan, her hair as unruly as a rag mop, chanting New Age gobbledegook about bad auras and unharmonious vibrations.

Tom leaned forward, his eyes intense. 'Look, I know I'm a sucker for a hard-luck story. But Kelly is different. I'm hoping she'll be part of the family and this will be a great opportunity for you to see how wonderful she is.'

Ben came to a grim decision. He had no choice, really. He'd never been able to stifle the part of Tom's character governed by good intentions, although he'd tried.

Mere talking wouldn't convince Tom to rethink his plan. His brother's easygoing demeanor disguised a steel backbone. And yet marriage was too serious an undertaking to allow for a mistake— Ben had learned that lesson the hard way.

He'd keep an eye on Kelly Evers all right, but as for her becoming Kelly Shepard he'd find a way to bring Tom to his senses before a wedding ever took place.

CHAPTER ONE

I CAN do this.

The patient's radial pulse beat faintly under the index and middle fingers on Kelly Evers's left hand. Poised to obtain the blood sample she needed, she held the heparinized syringe in her right hand like a pencil with the needle an inch above the skin. Yet every time she thought she'd found her target the steady thump in the woman's wrist seemed to disappear.

The medium-sized pair of gloves didn't help matters either. Her fingers drowned inside the too-large protective gear, taking away nearly all of her tactile ability. She might as well be wearing woolen mittens.

Perspiration trickled between her breasts and she fought an urge to wipe her brow. Her heart pounded furiously, making her question whether the beat she was tracking with her fingertips was her patient's or her own.

Kelly took a deep breath. She *could* do this. It didn't matter that it had been years since she'd drawn an arterial blood gas. She knew the procedure. It was like riding a bike. Once you knew how you never forgot. You might be shaky at first, but the skill was there.

If only she could refresh her rusty technique under less critical circumstances, and without having a roomful of people witnessing her attempt.

Actually, it wasn't the presence of three nurses, bustling around the bedside, the two volunteer emergency medical technicians who'd brought the comatose forty-five-year-old female in the Sundance city ambulance or the radiology technician, standing by with his portable X-ray unit, who caused her to feel like a greenhorn.

It was Dr Ben Shepard who, with his stormy blue-gray eyes, transported her back to the days of being an insecure twenty-one-year-old medical technology student. Funny thing—his brother Tom had always treated her like a valued colleague, not a subservient underling.

She didn't like the change in status at all.

Still, she was glad that her co-worker had taken the other blood samples back to the lab and was already in the middle of processing them.

The thready pulse beneath her fingers stabilized. Kelly squared her shoulders, ready to push the needle into the artery, but a deep, melodic bass voice from above broke her concentration.

'Will we get those blood gas results some time before the chopper flies in from Rapid City? It's due in about ten minutes, you know.'

His faint note of sarcasm sent another wave of heat through her. 'I'm doing my best.'

'See if you can do your best a little faster, will you?'

Grimly, she refocused on her task. It was now or never. She plunged the needle into the skin exposed between her two fingers. The satisfying pop didn't occur and the syringe remained empty.

Her heart sank to her toes and her temperature rose to overheated levels.

'Have you done this before?' Dr Shepard snapped.

Innate honesty compelled her to tell the truth. 'Yes, but it was a long time ago.'

Before she could move a muscle a muttered oath drifted down upon her ears. 'Step aside.'

She held her ground, refusing to relinquish her hold in spite of the closeness of his body or his brusque order. 'I can do this,' she insisted, gently repositioning the needle in an effort to locate the artery. The pulse beat under her fingertips and she couldn't understand how she had missed the mark.

'I'm sure you can, but time is a luxury Connie Peterson doesn't have. She's not responding and I can't explain why. If we're going to save her I need every possible piece of information.'

One of the nurses interrupted. 'Fingerstick glucose is normal—one ten.'

'Vital signs appear normal. Respirations are down. No visible signs of trauma,' someone else reported.

Ben continued his lecture. 'The EMTs reported a seizure in the ambulance. I need your test results and I need them *now*.'

'No signs of needle tracks. According to her husband, no history of drug abuse,' another nurse reported in a calm voice. 'No prescription meds either.'

The syringe remained empty. Kelly didn't have a choice—she had to defer to his superior skill.

She hated the idea that he was right. Mrs Peterson didn't have time to be Kelly's guinea pig. More important, she hated her inability to accomplish her given task—*any* given task.

She pulled out the needle and placed a pressure pad over the site. Keeping her fingers on the cotton to stop any potential bleeding, she straightened and pointedly stepped aside without a word.

Inwardly, however, her heart sank. She'd wanted—*needed*—to demonstrate her competence to the staff at her newest temporary assignment. With any luck, it would become a permanent one, provided she could demonstrate a competence in every aspect of her job. Incidents like this would diminish her chances to a considerable degree.

And yet she couldn't fault him for taking over. The

patient came first, her ego a dim second. His attitude, however, made failure taste like bitter medicine.

The radiology tech positioned Mrs Peterson's head for the skull X-rays while the nurses continued to report their observations aloud. In spite of the activity around her, Kelly focused her gaze on Dr Shepard's lean fingers and neatly trimmed nails, taking in his thick russet-colored hair as he bent his head over their patient.

He was a large man, tall and broad of shoulder with a muscular sturdiness that Tom's gangly form lacked. Even with his body stooped over as he worked at his task, Ben dwarfed her in size. She didn't doubt that he towered over most men, including his six-foot-two-inch brother.

From her vantage point to his right, his face had the same strong bone structure of his younger sibling, but Ben's features possessed a more rugged edge. The lines around his eyes testified to Tom's casually mentioned ten-year age difference.

He wore a solid gray dress shirt with the end of his Windsor-knotted tie tucked inside the buttoned edges for safekeeping. The tie itself was a jarring shade of purple and featured a bald eagle with its outstretched wings soaring over snow-capped majestic mountains. The scene wasn't so bad, but the color... Considering the conservative nature of his shirt and black trousers, it seemed rather unusual for him to express such a unique taste in his accessories.

During her ruminations, which occurred in the blink of an eye, he inserted the needle into the patient's brachial artery near the bend of her elbow. He apparently preferred that site to the one she had chosen. With grudging admiration she watched as bright red blood pushed the plunger of the syringe upward, seemingly like magic.

After the syringe contained several milliliters of fluid he removed the needle, stuck the beveled edge into a rubber cork so the sample wouldn't be contaminated by any atmospheric oxygen, then pressed a cotton pad over the site in swift, competent motions.

He handed her the syringe. 'Thank you,' she murmured, berating herself once again for her failure as she rolled the sample between her hands to ensure the anticoagulant and blood were well mixed. As he straightened she noticed how her head barely came to the top of his broad shoulders and how her gaze met the painted stare of the bald eagle's.

He turned away, pointedly addressing the X-ray tech. 'How are we coming on those films?'

'Ready to go as soon as you folks step out of the way,' Vern, a young man of Kelly's age, said cheerfully.

Kelly grabbed the sample and the tray containing her supplies, then rushed from the trauma room toward the ideally located lab—down the hall and around the corner from ER.

As she hurried along she characterized Ben Shepard as rude and domineering—a total opposite to his brother's friendly and compassionate nature. She wondered if any of the nursing staff had succumbed to the urge to choke him with his own tie or if she was the only one to experience such a strong desire.

Kelly crossed the threshold of the small lab, carrying the blood gas sample reverently. At the same time her tension lifted at the prospect of being in safe, friendly territory once again.

Melody Carter, otherwise known as Dee, smiled at her. 'And you were afraid you wouldn't be able to collect the sample. I knew the know-how would come back to you. You just needed to build your confidence.'

'Actually, I missed. Dr Shepard drew the sample for

me. I don't think he was too happy about it either,' Kelly
added ruefully. She rolled the syringe between her hands
for several seconds, before injecting the well-mixed
blood into the analyzer.

Dee brushed away Kelly's comments with a wave of
her hand. 'It happens to the best of us,' the sixty-three-
year-old technician pronounced. 'Dr Shepard gets a little
testy when he's worried about his patients but he's a
great doctor and the nicest man you'll ever meet.'

Kelly wasn't so sure she agreed with the latter half of
her statement, but decided not to offer her opinion.

'Such a shame that he's had so many family troubles.'
Dee shook her head in obvious dismay. 'I'm hoping
some nice woman will come along and shake him out
of his bachelorhood. He's too young to live such a solitary life.'

Kelly's smile was wan. She didn't have any hopes or
dreams of attempting to change his or anyone else's mar-
ital status. A long time ago, six years in fact, she'd held
out for someone special—her personal hero—and had
been fooled by a little attention from a smooth talker.
Although she didn't regret the brief interlude which had
resulted in her daughter, Carlie, she certainly didn't intend to find herself in the same situation again. She'd
proven that she was a lousy judge of character and, because of her shortcoming, she wouldn't risk giving
Carlie a deadbeat stepfather to match her deadbeat dad.

'Does he always wear such weird ties?' Kelly asked.

Dee grinned. 'No. The hospital communications committee came up with "Bad Tie Day". If you'll notice,
all the men are wearing their wildest. We're supposed
to vote and the winner gets a free lunch in the cafeteria.'

Kelly laughed, thinking of the renowned quality of
hospital food. 'True incentive.'

'Yeah, well, it's something to boost morale. We just had "Strange Sock Day". I won,' Dee added proudly.

'Congratulations.'

Numbers flashed on the digital display screen and the printer tape advanced with the results. Kelly studied the figures and, seeing the low percentage of oxygen in Mrs Peterson's blood, knew they'd had good reason for inserting an airway.

'I'm just about finished if you want to wait a second and call everything at once,' Dee directed.

Kelly took the paper, dialed ER's extension and reported their findings to a nurse who sounded harried.

'Thanks,' Cheryl Rowe, the forty-seven-year-old ER supervisor, said. 'Mrs Peterson is leaving right now.'

Curiosity drove Kelly to ask, 'What's her diagnosis?'

'Possible cerebrovascular hemorrhage. Can't say for sure until they run a CT scan.'

Kelly thanked her and, after breaking the connection, repeated the nurse's statement.

Dee sighed at the news. 'It doesn't sound good for someone so young.'

Kelly agreed. Having a daughter of her own, she wondered if Mrs Peterson had any children. The thought of a child losing his or her mother sent a shiver of apprehension down her spine.

'Do you see a lot of situations requiring an emergency airlift?' she asked. After starting the job at Sundance Community Hospital two days earlier on June first, she was trying to get a feel for the duties she'd be performing over the next several months.

Dee shrugged. 'It runs in spells. We handle minor emergencies all the time. The major cases only stay long enough for the doctors to stabilize the patient. We have periods where we transfer everyone out as fast as they come into ER.'

'What about surgery and OB?'

'They leave by regular ambulance for Spearfish, which is thirty miles away. Cardiac patients and the folks needing other specialists travel on to Rapid City, which is an hour's drive to the east. Once in a while we have to call for a helicopter. Depends on the situation.'

Kelly recalled the information she'd received in her orientation packet. Sundance Community served the five thousand plus county residents, including their twelve hundred city dwellers, with three family practice physicians, two physician's assistants and a nurse-practitioner who provided a basic range of medical services.

The facility's referral system kicked into gear to meet the people's more complicated needs. The medical staff automatically passed along any questionable case for further evaluation, and a variety of consultants held daily clinics for follow-up care and ordinary office calls.

All things considered, this was a nice change from her last assignment at a clinic lab where 'routine' had been the order of the day. And yet she'd thought the pace too fast for the three lab employees—one of them an absentee boss.

As the hours passed the ER staff required her services far more than she'd expected. Luckily, none of the cases were as dramatic as Connie Peterson's, but trepidation that she might encounter Ben Shepard again filled her soul each time she crossed the department's threshold. She doubted if he'd understand how anyone could suffer from 'new job' jitters.

What a shame that he was so different from Tom. Love truly is blind, she thought to herself, remembering the heart-warming stories Tom had related about his older brother. The picture he'd painted didn't resemble the Ben Shepard she'd met.

Still, she'd give Ben the benefit of the doubt. Any

sibling of Tom's had to possess at least *some* good qualities. Stressful ER conditions didn't bring out the best in people and she'd had her own share of bad days.

The rest of her shift passed by uneventfully but, even so, when six o'clock rolled around she was ready to leave.

'Big evening planned?' Dee asked.

Kelly shook her head. 'I have a few more things to unpack. I also promised Carlie we'd visit the park tonight and have a picnic.'

'At least the weather's nice enough. How does she like the day-care center?'

Kelly grimaced, thinking of the stubborn set to her daughter's jaw as they'd left the house that morning. 'OK, I guess. She's still in the adjustment period.'

'Making friends is tough,' Dee commiserated, 'but Susannah Whipple is great for making new arrivals feel welcome.'

Kelly hoped so. After they parted company she drove toward the center, anxious to see her daughter.

Inside the brightly painted child-friendly building, she walked toward Carlie's room, wearing a smile of anticipation. She'd see her five-year-old's sweet smile and her reddish-blonde hair in perpetual disarray, feel her enthusiastic hugs and the wet kisses and hear about the fun things she'd done to fill her day.

Peering through the open door into the playroom, her excitement faded. Carlie sat on a bench in one corner, hugging her stuffed Dalmatian to her chest and kicking her legs aimlessly in the air. Her Cupid's-bow mouth was turned into a frown and her shoulders were slumped in obvious misery.

Carlie's unhappiness seared Kelly's heart. From her lone position in the corner it was painfully apparent that she had shunned the other children. Kelly could already hear Carlie's monotone as she dutifully recited her activities, exhibiting emotion only through her heartfelt plea to stay with Kelly the next day.

At each place they'd moved to in the last year Carlie's circle of friends had grown smaller and smaller in spite of Kelly's best efforts to encourage her daughter's relationships. With this move Carlie didn't express any interest in meeting new playmates—a point of concern for Kelly.

Apparently their nomadic lifestyle was taking its toll. Suspecting this some months ago, Kelly had been actively searching for a full-time, permanent position. Unfortunately, the available jobs were either part time or covered those hours when Carlie would be home from school. The prospect of never seeing Carlie except on the weekends was totally unacceptable and, consequently, she'd ignored those so-called opportunities.

And yet the day was fast approaching when she wouldn't have the luxury of a choice. Carlie would begin kindergarten in September—a mere three months away—and Kelly had vowed to make her daughter's school years stable ones.

Putting her in a new learning environment every three months was unthinkable. If this job didn't pan out into a permanent appointment Kelly had only one option left—one too painful to consider.

Still, miracles did happen and Kelly's was long overdue.

A youthful Susannah Whipple—a woman who'd earned an advanced degree in early childhood education and mothered two elementary school girls—approached. Her unhurried movements spoke of her calm temperament and good nature in dealing with the rambunctious leaders of tomorrow.

'How did it go today?' Kelly asked in a low voice.

'Not bad. She spent more time playing with the others than by herself. Be patient. It's only Wednesday.'

Just then Carlie glanced toward the door. The smile that spread across her face reminded Kelly of the sun, breaking out from behind a cloud. Carlie jumped off the bench and ran forward, her arms outstretched. 'Mommy!'

Kelly hugged her daughter close as she stroked her fine hair. 'Hi sweetie. How was your day?'

'Fine,' she responded noncommittally. 'Can we go now?'

'You bet. But first let's tell your friends goodbye.'

Carlie's hand clung to hers as if she feared being left behind. Susannah flashed them both a smile. 'See you in the morning, Carlie.' She added in a low voice, for Kelly's ears only, 'Tomorrow will be better. Don't worry.'

Kelly nodded at the now-familiar parting statement, hoping—praying—the woman's prediction would come to pass. It killed her inside to see Carlie's vivacious personality becoming dim, and she could only hope that Sundance, Wyoming, would be the place where she could reverse the process.

'See you, then,' Kelly said in a too-bright voice.

Carlie tugged on her hand. 'Let's go *now*, Mommy.'

She walked beside Kelly as they headed toward the used mini-van which carried all of their worldly possessions as they migrated around the country.

'What would you like to eat on our picnic?' Kelly asked once they'd buckled the seat belts and started on the short drive to their two-bedroom rental house.

'Peanut butter and jelly,' Carlie promptly replied. 'With soda pop and chocolate ice cream and a whole bag of Oreos and corn chips.'

Kelly smiled at her daughter's menu, consisting of her

favorite snack foods. 'How about fried chicken, fruit juice, carrot sticks and *two* Oreos?'

'No ice cream?'

Unswayed by Carlie's plaintive note, Kelly only said, 'We'll see.'

After Kelly changed clothes she loaded a picnic blanket, lightweight jackets and her sketch pad into the van, before they stopped at Sundance's grocery store for their supper. In no time at all they had selected the ideal picnic spot near the Imagination Station. Similar to the massive play structures for kids at fast-food chains, it featured enclosed lookout sections at each of the four corners, in addition to slides and a suspended bridge.

While Kelly unpacked the basket of food Carlie plopped onto the blanket, sitting yoga-style. 'I'm hungry.'

'I am too,' Kelly agreed.

A minute later, the sound of childish voices caught her attention. She glanced toward the basketball court about fifty feet away where two boys played a game of one-on-one. The younger of the pair lost control of the ball and it bounced off the concrete. The two went in pursuit but the larger boy, husky, brown-haired and approximately twelve, shoved his smaller, dark-headed companion and sent him sprawling on the grass.

The victim—about nine years old, Kelly guessed— cried out in dismay. Kelly's maternal instinct shouted a warning and she rose to watch the unfolding events, ready to intervene if necessary. The boys now began to wrestle over a baseball cap and the basketball lay in the grass, apparently forgotten.

Carlie's gaze followed her mother's. 'Those boys aren't playing very nice,' she announced importantly.

'No, dear. They're not.' Kelly glanced around in case

the parents were close by. The park was empty, making her the only adult in the near vicinity.

The smaller one staggered to his feet, his fists raised. The bully punched at his face and the child held his nose as he fell again. From her location, Kelly could hear the older boy's taunts.

'Come on, Troy. I wanna see what you can do, ya little snot-nosed wimp.'

Her ire grew. Being small of stature, she'd suffered at the hands of those larger than herself on more than one occasion and it galled her to see it happen before her eyes. Enough was enough.

She jumped to her feet. 'Don't move from this spot,' she instructed Carlie. 'I'll be right back.'

Without waiting for Carlie's acknowledgement she rushed into the fray. 'Stop it! Stop it right now.'

The husky boy stared at her with insolent eyes and sneered, clearly not intimidated by her order. 'You gonna stop me?'

Troy lay at his feet, curled into a fetal position. His surrender, however, didn't prevent the bully from kicking the child's legs. 'That'll teach you to make me mad.'

Troy cried out. Kelly's anger grew to volcanic proportions and she stepped between the tyrant and his victim. Part of her brain registered that he matched her in size and was probably a lot stronger, but she refused to show any fear.

She pushed him away, giving Troy time to rise and retreat. 'You should be ashamed of yourself.'

He shoved her back. 'Hey, lady, mind your own business.'

Adrenaline made her hold her ground. 'Not while you're picking on someone smaller than yourself. What's your name?'

He shoved her again. 'I ain't telling you.'

She poked a finger in his chest. 'That's OK. I'll just give your description to the police. They'll know who you are.'

Cockiness exuded from him. 'Think so?'

Troy ran around her, clearly intent on attacking his adversary's unprotected side. The older one staggered backwards a few steps, then began to swing with clenched fists.

Caught between the two opponents, Kelly attempted to separate them. Before she could grab hold of the flailing arms pain shot through her chest. Her lungs emptied.

Fighting for breath, she crumpled to her knees.

CHAPTER TWO

A HUNDRED yards from the scene, Ben saw the petite strawberry blonde wade into the fight. It was the same lady who'd dwelled in his thoughts all day, the one he'd hoped to exorcise from his mind during his evening run.

Anticipating trouble, he increased his jog to a sprint. 'Fool woman,' he muttered under his breath. Halfway to his destination he watched helplessly as Deke Anderson's fist drove Kelly to her knees.

He called out in his most authoritative tone. 'Hold it right there.'

His words echoed through the clearing, like a thunderbolt from heaven, and instantly the combatants froze. The older one—the instigator, Ben supposed—glanced around. At the sight of Ben, bearing down on him, a look of panic crossed his face and he pivoted to race away in the opposite direction.

'Percy! Guard!'

Ben's Dalmatian raced toward his quarry. Percy, his teeth bared, dogged the boy's steps until he'd effectively pinned him against a nearby tree trunk.

Confident in Percy's guarding abilities, Ben knelt beside Kelly and scanned her for obvious injuries. No longer clad in the white lab coat, she wore a pair of denim shorts and a lavender cotton blouse. The top three buttons were undone, revealing the lacy edge of her undergarment and the burgeoning swell of her breasts.

He swallowed hard. Remembering his brother's claim on her, he forced his gaze to her face. 'Are you OK?'

She bobbed her head. 'L-lost my…breath. I'm…fine.

Ch-check him.' She motioned to the youngster beside her.

Troy's eyes were huge with fright as blood continued to stream out of his nostrils in spite of his attempts to stem the flow. 'Pinch your nose and tilt your head back,' Ben instructed.

The boy obeyed. Ben took a closer look, recognizing him as one of his patients. 'Troy Davis, right?'

'Uh-huh.' Troy nodded for emphasis.

'Do your folks know where you are?'

'Yes.' The child's voice held a distinctly nasal quality.

Ben unhooked the cellular phone from the waist of his athletic shorts and punched a number from memory. 'Trudi, Ben Shepard. Ask one of the patrol cars to drive by the park. I have a couple of young men who were disturbing the peace and need an escort home.'

'Sure thing.' Trudi's unflappable manner and a perpetual wad of gum in her mouth made her the perfect candidate for the dispatcher position. 'Let me guess. Was one of them Deke Anderson?'

Ben glanced at Percy's prisoner. 'Yes.' After disconnecting the call, he reattached the phone to his waistband. 'How's the nose?'

Troy lowered his head and Ben gently examined his face. 'A little swollen, but not bad. You'll probably look like a raccoon for a few days.'

'My mom's gonna kill me,' he moaned, unaffected by Ben's attempt to lighten the situation.

'What happened?' Ben asked.

'He started it,' Deke bellowed. Between Ben's glare and Percy's bark, he quieted down.

Troy pointed to a high branch. 'He threw my cap up there when I wouldn't give it to him. It's my Atlanta Braves baseball cap—the one my aunt sent me for my birthday.'

'If I get his stupid cap, can I go?' Deke whined.

Ben chose not to be magnanimous. 'Sorry. You'll have to wait for the police to get here.'

He turned toward Kelly, and noticed her daughter, running toward them. At least he assumed the child was her daughter—she was small-framed and had the same elfin features, hair color and curly, shoulder-length style as her mother.

'The police will want your statement,' he said, ignoring the twinge of jealousy he felt at seeing Kelly embrace the little girl.

'I understand.' She rose, her daughter still plastered to her side.

He noticed how Kelly barely reached the middle of his chest. She would be about five feet two, but her eyes weren't blue, as the song said. They were hazel.

A patrol car screeched to a stop and a tall, burly man unfolded himself from behind the wheel. 'Hear you found some trouble, Ben,' Officer Tompkins called out as he approached the small gathering.

'Just happened to be in the right place at the right time, Al,' Ben said. 'Apparently there's a property dispute.' He pointed to the overhead branch.

Tompkins's gaze traveled upwards. 'I see.' He pulled out his notepad and began to jot down Ben's and Kelly's version of events. Then, after the article in question had been retrieved and after Ben had released Percy from guard duty, Tompkins said, 'Well, now, boys, let's go for a ride. We'll talk on the way.' Gripping the protesting Deke's arm, he ushered the two boys to his vehicle.

Ben turned his attention to Kelly. Conscious of her daughter's presence only a few feet away, he upbraided her actions in a quiet but cold voice. 'I hope you'll show better judgement before you jump in the middle of another dispute.'

Kelly appeared affronted. 'Better judgement?'

'Yes. Deke Anderson is trouble.'

'It's too bad someone didn't clue me in about him when we moved to town.' Her sarcasm was obvious. 'I had no idea that Sundance's citizens allowed juvenile delinquents to roam the streets, unsupervised.'

Her censure struck home and he softened his harsh tone. 'All I'm saying is for you to be careful. I may not be around to save you next time.'

She visibly bristled and her eyes flashed. Apparently, the reddish highlights in her hair didn't come close to the sparks in her personality. 'Save me? I didn't need or ask for your help.'

He scoffed. 'You weren't in any condition to ask. Regardless, you got it anyway. Deke's put two boys in the hospital over the past few months. You were lucky. He only knocked the air out of you.'

Her eyes widened in momentary alarm before she recovered. 'Then I'm glad I was here to divert his attention from Troy.' She continued in the next breath. 'For your information, if I see two boys engaged in a mismatched fight I'll jump in again.'

'I don't doubt it,' he said wryly. No wonder Tom had asked him to keep an eye on Kelly Evers. Twice today he'd rescued Ms Evers from situations where she was clearly out of her depth. In his opinion she now had two strikes against her.

She was too much like his helpless ex-wife, depending on him to make every decision or to extricate her from unpleasant circumstances. At first he'd been flattered by Alyce's dependence, but it had soon palled. If his brother wasn't bright enough to learn from his mistakes then Ben would take matters into his own hands.

It was his duty, borne out of love and concern for his brother, to save Tom from a similar life experience.

A tug on the hem of his T-shirt caught his attention. He glanced down at the little girl clutching a stuffed animal in one hand. A knot formed in his chest as his memories formed a bitter-sweet picture of his own daughter at this age. Tanya had always grabbed his pants leg to get his attention.

'I'm Carlie. What's your name?' she asked.

'Ben. Ben Shepard.'

'*Dr* Shepard,' Kelly corrected.

Carlie held out her spotted creature. 'Your dog looks like my Perdita.'

Without thinking, he glanced at Percy who had ferreted out a grasshopper and was busy chasing it across the grass. 'He does,' Ben agreed.

'What's *his* name?' she asked in a sing-song voice.

'Percy.' The animal's ears perked in response. Then, as no other command came forth, he returned to scouting the vicinity with his nose low to the ground.

'Oh. Want to change it to Pongo?'

He grinned. 'Would you like it if your mom called you something different?'

She wrinkled her face, clearly pondering the idea. ''Pends on what it was. I'd have to like it.'

'Percy's used to his name. He might not like being called Pongo.'

'Oh. You'd better keep it, then.' Carlie sighed. 'But if he has puppies, can one of them be a Pongo?'

His smile grew apologetic at her hopeful expression. 'Percy won't have puppies. He's a boy.'

'Oh.' She paused, clearly considering this new piece of information. 'Well if he's ever a daddy—'

Kelly interrupted. 'That's enough, Carlie. Dr Shepard doesn't have time to discuss all the possibilities with you.' She tilted her head up to meet his gaze. 'Carlie likes to think of all the angles. Sometimes it's hard to stay one step ahead of her.'

Having seen the intelligence shining out of Carlie's clear blue eyes, he could imagine Kelly's difficulties in dealing with a precocious child on her own. No wonder she'd set her sights on Tom. Thinking of his brother, he hardened the portion of his heart that had started thawing towards her.

In a split second Kelly noticed the atmosphere had changed. Tension now sparked the air. Puzzled over what had caused it, she felt ill at ease. Before she could extricate herself from the situation Carlie tugged on her shirt.

'I'm hungry, Mommy. Can we eat?'

Grateful for the interruption, Kelly smiled at her. 'You bet.'

Carlie stared into Ben's face. 'It's Mother's Day and we're having a picnic. Want to eat with us?'

While Kelly waited with baited breath for his reply the harsh lines around his mouth softened. 'Maybe next time.'

'OK.' Carlie moved away to study a nearby dandelion.

'Mother's Day?' Ben was clearly puzzled. 'We're not celebrating it twice this year, are we?'

Kelly grinned. 'Several years ago I stopped at a restaurant for a bucket of fried chicken and since the weather was beautiful we ate it at the park. Carlie was in the ''why'' stage at the time so I explained how mommies sometimes liked to have a day where they didn't cook. In her mind she associated it with Mother's Day. Now every picnic is ''Mother's Day''.'

Ben chuckled and the previous tension evaporated. 'Then I won't keep you any longer.'

Carlie's high-pitched giggles caught her attention.

Kelly's peace, however, turned to worry at the sight of her daughter, racing toward the Dalmatian. In the next instant she flung her arms around Percy's neck.

Fear clogged Kelly's throat and she bolted forward. She'd observed the animal's protective instincts in action and didn't want Carlie to get bitten because Percy had misinterpreted her friendly gesture.

'Caroline Marie Evers! What have I told you about getting too close to strange dogs?'

Ben's long strides brought him beside her. 'He won't hurt her.'

'Yes, but she doesn't know that,' Kelly snapped. 'Just because she likes dogs, Dalmatians in particular, doesn't mean she should—'

'Jump into the middle of a potentially dangerous situation?' he asked pointedly.

'That's right.' She bobbed her head for emphasis.

He grabbed her elbow, pinning her to the spot. 'Carlie and Percy are fine. Don't make an issue of it.'

Kelly glared at him, wishing for her highest heels to minimize the distance between them. 'Don't make an issue of it? I'm trying to teach my daughter restraint so she won't get bitten or mauled and you're telling me not to *make an issue of it*?'

'Exactly.'

'Is that one of the child-rearing techniques you learned in medical school?'

He didn't respond to her sarcasm. 'No. It's simply an observation. You can't scold her about impetuous behavior when she sees you doing the same thing.'

'Impetuous behavior?' she sputtered. The urge to kick him in the shins grew stronger.

He nodded. 'Remember Deke?'

Her ire deflated like a popped balloon.

A wry twist appeared at the corners of his mouth. 'Need I say more?'

It galled her to admit that he was probably right. She crossed her arms and planted her sneaker-clad feet apart. 'Be that as it may, I can't believe you'd want me to turn my back on a bully, beating the tar out of someone who clearly can't defend himself.'

'Deke is as big as you are. Did you think you could physically stop him?'

'I was more concerned about Troy.'

'And you should have been,' he agreed. 'But after Deke incapacitated you he could have easily gone after Troy again.'

'But he didn't.'

He heaved a sigh. 'Look, we could debate this all night. I'm simply saying that you should have called for help before you tried to break up a fight, involving a youth who outweighs you.'

Grudgingly, she conceded the point.

'If you don't own a cellular phone get one,' he ordered. 'You may never encounter a similar situation but, being a single parent, you and Carlie can't afford to be stranded. You've read the newspapers. Terrible things can happen if you're not prepared.'

She gritted her teeth at his censuring tone. The fragile peace between them had shattered. 'I'll take your advice under consideration.'

'I hope so.' He whistled to Percy, but the dog didn't respond to his summons. 'Come, Percy!' he demanded.

The dog hesitated as he glanced between his master and Carlie, then walked towards Ben with obvious reluctance. Kelly took great pleasure in the sight. Even the man's *dog* didn't want to spend time in his company, she thought.

'Does Percy have to leave?' Carlie asked.

'Yes, he does, sweetie.'

'Can I play with him again, Dr Ben?'

'We'll see,' was his noncommittal reply. Ben faced Kelly. 'By the way, did you find everything at the house in working order?'

'I ran across a few glitches, but nothing I couldn't handle.' Having encountered her share of absentee landlords who only appeared to collect the rent, she'd learned a few do-it-yourself tricks over the years. The manual she'd purchased had paid for itself several times.

'Good. If you need anything call the Powder River Real Estate agency. They rent the place for me and are responsible for maintenance.'

'*If* something comes along that I can't handle, I will.'

His raised eyebrow indicated that he'd noted her emphasis on the word 'if'. 'Enjoy your picnic.' With that he set off at a jog, with Percy following.

As he disappeared around a bend Kelly wondered why Tom had instructed her to deal with Ben if a problem arose when Ben so obviously didn't want to be bothered. No matter. Asking Ben Shepard for help of any kind was the last thing she intended to do.

A week later, Kelly stared at the rising water level in the bathtub with dismay. The drain was clogged and the faucet handle had broken off while in the 'on' position. Water spewed forth at full speed. Her only choice to prevent a household flood was to completely shut off the supply at the water main until someone repaired the fixture.

Unfortunately, its location was a mystery. Even if she knew where it was she didn't have the proper tools.

Her hand throbbed in time to her rapid heart rate. During her attempt to fix the perpetual drip she'd gashed the fleshy part of her palm. Instead of the minor repair job that she'd performed countless times before, a disaster loomed.

To add insult to injury, the real estate agency had closed hours ago and now she had to call Ben. Trouble always seemed to come in threes, but why did each of her problems involve Ben Shepard in some way?

She didn't want him, or anyone else, rescuing her. She'd worked long and hard these past five years to be self-sufficient, and she wouldn't let those years go to waste. Her mother might enjoy a life of dependence, but it wasn't the life Kelly wanted for herself or her daughter.

Carlie peered over her shoulder. Clapping her hands, she jumped up and down on the linoleum in her bare feet. 'Mommy! We got a swimming pool!'

'Yes, but don't get in,' Kelly ordered. Water would soon spill over the sides of the tub on its own; it didn't need Carlie's help.

She plucked Carlie's play bucket off the floor and handed it to her. 'Start bailing.'

Carlie grabbed the blue plastic toy. 'What does "bail" mean?'

'Dip the bucket into the bathtub. Then dump the water into the sink,' said Kelly, as she wrapped a towel around her bleeding hand. 'I'm going to call Dr Shepard.'

'OK.' Carlie began to work, engrossed in her task. Hopefully, her efforts would buy them some time.

Kelly dashed into the kitchen and flipped the pages of the phone book to the Ss. She hated to call him when he'd made it plain that he wasn't to be bothered, but she didn't have a choice.

After memorizing his number, she squared her shoulders and punched the seven digits. With any luck, she'd find him at home and not at the hospital in the middle of a medical crisis.

'Hello.' The man's familiar gruff voice needed no identification.

'Where is the main water shut-off valve?' The words tumbled out of her mouth.

'Kelly?' His voice sounded incredulous.

'Yes,' she said a trifle impatiently. 'I have a plumbing problem, and unless you tell me where the main water valve is in the next few seconds you can advertise your house as Sundance's newest swimming pool.'

'I'll be there in ten minutes.'

A click preceded the dial tone and she wanted to scream with frustration. 'That's not what I asked for,' she told the receiver, before slamming it onto its cradle.

She rushed into the bathroom. 'How're you doing?'

'Fine.' Carlie dipped into the tub again and dumped her few ounces of water down the sink. Water lapped at the edges of the porcelain tub and Carlie's collection of plastic yellow ducks floated with wild abandon across the turbulent surface. Sighing with resignation, Kelly grabbed a utility bucket and began bailing.

After a few minutes she began to tire, but she considered this chore more attractive than the alternative of mopping gallons of water off the floor. If she was lucky Ben would arrive before her endurance failed.

'Is Dr Ben coming?' Carlie tossed a plastic mermaid into the tub to join the ducks—an action making her more of a hindrance than a help.

'Yes.' Kelly heaved another bucket over the sink and poured out its contents. 'Don't put in any more toys,' she ordered, trying not to sound as exasperated as she felt. 'Please.'

'OK. Will he bring Percy?'

'I don't know.'

'Can I go watch for him?'

'Yes, you may.'

Permission granted, Carlie skipped from the room. Kelly continued her ritual, using her left hand as her right palm burned. Water sloshed out of the bathtub and bucket, soaking her in the process. Frustrated by her clumsy efforts, and unused to such frantic manual labor, her shoulders began to ache. Just as she considered the battle lost Carlie's voice drifted into the room.

'Dr Ben's here!'

Thank goodness, Kelly thought.

A few seconds later the water, gushing out of the spigot, slowed to a trickle, then mere drops.

Kelly emptied three more buckets of water for good measure, delaying their meeting as long as possible. Finally she straightened, steeling herself for the censure she'd find in his stormy blue-gray eyes. She squared her shoulders and turned to find Ben's large frame, filling the doorway.

He blinked and his face took on a shocked expression.

Her stomach somersaulted. 'I can explain,' she began.

Ben stared at Kelly, totally unprepared for the sight of her wet blouse, molding generous curves, or the semi-transparency of the cotton fabric.

She might be child-sized, but she was definitely a woman.

Dark circles dotted her denim shorts—shorts that revealed a long expanse of tanned and slender legs.

Her curly shoulder-length hair, neatly restrained on his previous encounters, now hung in wet ringlets around her oval face.

As he struggled to bring his errant thoughts and raging hormones under control he noticed the bloodstained towel wrapped around her hand.

'What happened?'

'I can explain,' she repeated, looking as if she expected his temper to explode and was bracing herself for the worst. 'I'm sorry about the water, but we managed to prevent any structural damage.'

He stepped into the bathroom. 'I'm not worried about the house.'

'You're not?' Her surprise made him feel shallow. He didn't like giving the impression of being more concerned over his property than people.

'I'm not,' he said firmly. 'What did you do to yourself?'

'Oh, this?' She waved her injured hand. 'I was repairing the faucet when—'

'The Realtor is supposed to deal with those problems,' he interrupted.

'I know, but the tub doesn't empty very well and the faucet leaks. Or it did,' she corrected, 'before all this happened. Anyway, when I came home from work I had a tubful of water so I decided to take care of the drip myself and let the agency deal with the clogged drain in the morning.'

He took her hand in his and began to unwrap the towel. 'But something went wrong.'

'Unfortunately,' she said wryly. 'When I took the handles off to check out the problem the pieces were so corroded that they literally disintegrated in my hands. The next thing I knew, water gushed out and a jagged edge sliced my palm.'

He cradled her upturned hand in his, feeling her soft skin and noting her small bone structure. He gently probed the long cut, running from the base of her thumb to her wrist, disturbed to see the blood welling up between the edges. 'You're going to need stitches.'

'A few butterfly bandages should be enough,' she protested as he rewrapped her palm.

'Sorry. I don't think so.'

'How about that new superglue stuff?'

He raised one dark eyebrow. 'Afraid of needles?'

'No. I just don't have time for a trip to the ER.'

'Too bad. Let's go.' He succumbed to an odd urge to touch her again. Clasping her elbow, he went to lead her out of the room.

However, she didn't budge. 'I can't leave Carlie and I don't want her sitting in the waiting room by herself. Besides, it's almost her bedtime.'

He gave her a fierce glare, but she didn't flinch under his strong-willed gaze. Her set jaw, stiff spine and defiant hazel eyes revealed her resolve to hold firm.

'What if I promise red-carpet treatment? You'll be in and out in fifteen minutes.'

Kelly shook her head.

He lifted his eyes in supplication. 'Somehow I knew she wouldn't be agreeable.' Meeting her gaze, he shrugged as he released her. 'OK, OK. I'll bring a suture kit to the house. Will that satisfy you?'

Her tense features relaxed. 'Yes.'

'I'll be back in a few minutes. Don't do anything in the meantime.'

She saluted. 'Yes, sir.'

Ben strode into the living room, not surprised to see Carlie playing with Percy. The dog rose as Ben headed towards the door. 'Stay,' he commanded. Perhaps Percy could keep both mother and daughter out of trouble.

Percy sat, his tongue hanging out in apparent satisfaction.

Halfway to the hospital Ben wondered if Tom had anticipated Kelly's propensity for disaster. How many more times would he have to rescue Kelly Evers?

CHAPTER THREE

KELLY dropped the armload of wet clothes and towels on top of the washing machine, before returning to the bathroom. 'Time to get out of the tub,' she announced.

Carlie surfaced, removing the snorkel from her mouth to speak. 'Do I have to?' Her lower chin quivered and her teeth chattered from the cold.

Kelly cast her a benevolent smile. Carlie loved to swim and wouldn't come out willingly. Perhaps Kelly's ace in the hole would stave off any forthcoming arguments. 'Percy's waiting for you.'

'Oh, yeah.' Carlie rose without protest and laid her toys on the tub's edge. Percy was definitely useful to have around if his presence brought forth co-operation.

Kelly held a pastel green bath towel at the ready and wrapped it around Carlie as soon as she stepped onto the mat. A tidal wave of water sloshed onto the floor.

Ignoring it for the moment, she towel-dried the light-colored locks plastered against Carlie's head. Ben was due back at any moment and she wanted to erase the traces of Carlie's swimming session before he returned. His instructions not to do anything surely didn't apply to helping her daughter prepare for bed, but she didn't want to take any chances.

She'd endured his scrutiny—and wrath—already today and wanted to forego enduring it again. The idea of being the recipient of his piercing gaze made her tense.

'Don't rub so hard, Mommy.'

'Sorry.' Kelly stopped her brisk one-handed motions and helped Carlie slip her yellow nightgown over her head. 'After you've combed your hair and brushed your teeth, you can keep Percy company.'

'OK.' Carlie raked her baby-fine hair while Kelly supervised her efforts. Although the part on the side of her head was crooked, Kelly deemed her daughter's efforts satisfactory.

Ignoring the ache in her hand, she began toweling the floor dry. Her movements were slow in spite of her determination to restore the bathroom before Ben returned.

'How can I brush my teeth without water?' Carlie asked.

The only liquid in the refrigerator was a bottle of orange juice, not satisfactory for the task at hand. 'I guess you'll have to skip it for now.' Missing one night surely wouldn't create a mouthful of cavities.

'Oh, boy!' Carlie scurried away, as if anxious to leave before her mother changed her mind.

Giving the linoleum one last swipe, Kelly thought she'd accomplished her objective. However, the sound of Ben clearing his throat made her triumph shortlived.

His squared jawline revealed his displeasure at her outright disobedience. Caught in her defiant act, a flash of heat spread across her face. She felt compelled to defend herself.

'I had to wipe up the water before someone slipped and hurt themselves. Besides, I used my good hand.' She staggered to her feet, clutching the two towels she'd used.

He advanced, making the bathroom—spacious by most standards—seem infinitely smaller. 'Tell me something. Do you always ignore the advice people give you, or is it just me?'

She lowered her gaze to the floor, chagrined. After discovering her pregnancy, she'd broken free from living under her father's thumb. From that moment on she'd made her own decisions—and mistakes. As for his order, she knew the importance of following a physician's directives but she also knew—as did they—that on occasion their suggestions were impractical and impossible to follow.

This was one of those times.

He folded his arms across his chest, as if waiting for her reply.

'Sorry,' she said, unrepentant. 'I wanted to follow your advice, but my daughter needed attention so I couldn't. It wasn't anything personal.'

His eyes lost their stormcloud appearance and his face relaxed. 'Good. Then you'll keep your hand dry and won't overwork it? I don't want the stitches tearing or becoming infected.'

She fidgeted under his gaze. 'I'll do my best, but the lab's extremely busy right now.'

'Do I have to officially curtail your activities?' he asked matter-of-factly.

'You wouldn't!'

'Try me.'

She stared at him, aghast. 'You're serious, aren't you?'

'Very much so.'

Sensing he wouldn't back down from his position, she capitulated. 'OK, OK. You win. I'll take good care of my hand. Now, can we get on with this?'

'Sure. Shall we do this in a place where we'll both be more comfortable?'

'Absolutely.' There wasn't a room in her house—his house, actually—where she could relax in his presence. Even so, the extra space in the kitchen should dilute his disconcerting effect on her.

She led the way to the table, sat in one of the chairs and began unwrapping her makeshift bandage. She could hear Carlie's high-pitched voice as she talked to Percy in the living room.

Ben opened his pack, created a sterile field on the surface and prepared his syringe of novocaine. He lifted her hand and placed it in his while he examined the gash.

Watching a needle enter her skin didn't bother her, but somehow the idea of thread piercing her flesh did. She closed her eyes and inhaled a bracing breath, willing herself to concentrate on something—*anything*—else.

The scent of a familiar brand of soap filled her nostrils, emphasizing the fact that he'd taken a shower and she hadn't.

Her mind wandered. She'd always imagined jogging alongside the man of her dreams, travelling down a tree-lined country lane like a pair of matched bays. Afterwards they'd enjoy a sensual interlude in an oversized hot tub, sipping Asti Spumante champagne and nibbling on strawberries.

Without conscious effort the doctor, holding her wrist, replaced her fantasy man. She could imagine his embrace—strong and protective, yet loose enough to allow her to act on her own. Nor would her opinions, her talents or her goals threaten her hero's self-worth.

His bare knee brushed against her exposed thigh. The hardness of his leg burned like fire against her, sending a warmth into her very center. Her body responded of its own volition and her pelvic muscles tensed. She shifted positions.

'Ready?' he asked.

Kelly opened her eyes, her gaze meeting his. His face hovered inches away, close enough for his breath to brush against her cheek. She studied his features, noticing the whiskery shadow on his chin in the seconds that seemed to last for ever.

She felt as if she were seeing him for the first time.

This wasn't Ben Shepard, the doctor. This was Ben Shepard, the man—with masculinity oozing out of every pore.

'What are you guys doin'?' Innocently curious, Carlie stood at the doorway. Percy poked his nose inside as if he, too, was interested in the adults' activities.

The magical spell shattered. Kelly leaned back, instinctively trying to pull her hand free. Although Ben straightened his posture he didn't release his hold.

She cleared her throat. 'Ben is taking care of my cut.'

'Oh.' Apparently satisfied by the comment, Carlie and the Dalmatian vanished as quickly as they'd appeared.

A sharp pain stung Kelly's palm. She flinched as Ben injected the anesthetic under her skin in several places. 'You could have warned me.'

'I did. Several minutes ago.'

'Are you this considerate of all of your patients or is it just me?' She spoke crossly as she parroted his earlier remark.

He grinned. It was a genuine smile—the first she'd ever seen on his face. 'All of my victims get my undivided attention.' He touched a part of her palm. 'Feel this?'

'No.'

'Good.' He placed her hand on the table, then tugged on a pair of latex gloves. After organizing his sterile supplies, he bent his head over her hand. 'Here we go.'

'Must you sound so cheerful about this?'

'Mmm, testy are we?'

'Yes.'

Ben gave her a knowing glance. 'So you're one of those people who can dish out pain but can't take it.'

'It isn't the pain that bothers me, it's the idea of sewing. Crazy, I know, but of all the medical procedures I can't stand to watch this particular one.'

'Then you don't want a running commentary?'

She shuddered. 'Please don't.'

'What a shame.' His grin contradicted the feigned disappointment in his voice. 'Most people find it helps.'

She felt a tug in her palm and stared at the far corner where the ceiling met the wall. 'Helps what?'

He paused to stare at her with a twinkle in his eyes. 'To take your mind off what's happening. What shall we talk about?'

Her mind seized on the first thing that came to her. 'Tell me about the boy in the park. Derek?'

'Deke,' he corrected. 'Deke is our local problem child. He comes from a successful family—his father's an attorney, his mother's a loan officer at the bank. The youngest son of three, he's the proverbial black sheep. His older brothers are role models at the school—excel in sports, debate, all that sort of thing.'

'And Deke doesn't.'

He shook his head. 'No. He works as hard at getting into trouble as his brothers do to win awards.'

'What will happen to him for tonight's episode?'

'Probably nothing. His father will step in, smooth things over with everyone, pay for any damages and Deke will go home, without taking responsibility for his actions.'

'What a shame.'

'Yeah, it is.' He fell silent, engrossed in his task.

For a few seconds his slow, steady breathing echoed in her ear. Needing a diversion from thinking of the man beside her rather than the procedure she was enduring, she asked, 'How is Mrs Peterson?'

'The latest report from Rapid City showed a brain aneurysm. It apparently had begun seeping, which is why she lapsed into a coma. The neurosurgeon is hopeful, but it's too soon to predict any outcome.'

'Does she have any family?'

'Husband. Two kids. One is ten, the other thirteen.' Without pausing for breath, he asked, 'How long have you known Tom?'

'About four months.'

He froze. The hemostat holding the suture needle hung in mid-air. 'That's all?'

'Yeah.' Remembering how Tom had befriended her during her stint at Sheridan, her voice softened. 'He's a great guy. You must be proud of him.'

'I am.' He tossed his suture needle and bloody gauze pads onto the sterile wrap. 'All done. See?'

She glanced at her palm. A neat row of eight perfectly formed stitches ran along the fleshy part of her thumb. 'Nice sewing.'

'Come to my office in about a week so I can torture you again when I remove them.'

He gathered up the evidence of his house call and rewrapped the package to return to the hospital for disposal. 'As for your water situation—'

'I'll call the agency first thing in the morning.'

Ben continued as if she hadn't interrupted. 'You can't stay here.'

'I can't?'

He shook his head. 'You don't have water. You can't get a drink, brush your teeth or do anything else.'

'We'll manage.'

'Don't be difficult.'

'I'm not. I can't afford a night in a motel.' She could, but she didn't want to dip into her small nest egg. She'd earmarked it to purchase a house in the near future, provided Lady Luck smiled on her.

'*I'll* pay for it.' Without giving her time to argue, he soon had the Powder River Motel desk clerk on the line and stated his request.

For a moment she waited and watched his reaction to the clerk's conversation. 'I see. Thanks, anyway,' he said, before replacing the receiver.

'No vacancies?' Kelly guessed.

He nodded, his mouth forming a hard line.

'Well, then, it's settled. We're not going anywhere.' She hadn't realized how much the prospect of a hot shower had appealed to her until the opportunity had slipped out of her grasp as fast as it had entered.

'N-no.' He drew out the word. 'No. You can't stay here.'

'We don't have a choice,' she reminded him. 'I don't know anyone well enough to ask for any favors.'

His gaze became intent. 'You don't need to. You'll come home with me.'

Her jaw dropped. 'You?'

'Yeah. It's the least I can do.' He sounded resigned rather than thrilled.

Conscious of appearances, especially in a small town, she shook her head. 'What will people think?'

'They'll think that I generously offered you a place for the night and rightly so since I'm the owner of the property you're renting,' he pointed out. 'Even the most critical busybody can't complain, with Carlie acting as chaperon. Besides, it's already late and you'll leave early in the morning. No one will ever realize what happened.'

'I suppose.' Somehow she wasn't convinced this new arrangement would pass by unnoticed. If it did Ben might appear as a benevolent landlord, but she'd appear as a conniving stranger. Realistically, however, the idea of staying in a house without water seemed ridiculous when a tailor-made opportunity to avoid such primitive conditions existed.

'Grab your stuff and let's go. It's nearly ten o'clock.'

His impatience spurred her into action. She grabbed

an overnight bag out of her closet and began to pack a change of clothes and other necessities for herself and Carlie.

She rushed into the living room to give Carlie her bedroom slippers, but Ben, standing to the left of the doorway, grabbed her arm to stop her. He placed a finger to his lips. 'Look.'

Carlie lay on the floor in front of the television, fast asleep. Serving as her pillow, Percy rested his head on his front paws, seemingly enjoying his new function. He raised his head and cocked it as if asking what he should do.

'Is Percy used to little kids?' Kelly whispered. 'I'm surprised he's allowing her to treat him like he's a toy.'

'I am too. He tolerates most children, but I've never seen him as fascinated as he is with Carlie. He's always been so protective of me that he hasn't formed any attachments to other people.'

She started forward to rescue Percy from Carlie's dead weight, but Ben laid a restraining hand on her shoulder. He bent down to speak in her ear. 'Don't wake her. I'll carry her to your van.'

Knowing she couldn't lift Carlie with her injury, Kelly nodded. She watched as Ben slid his hands under Carlie's little body and raised her in his arms, his muscles scarcely straining under his light load. The care he paid her daughter, and the way Carlie snuggled against his chest, brought a lump of emotion to Kelly's throat.

She'd always dreamed of being part of a happy family unit, of Carlie's father playing an important role.

Unfortunately, the man she'd considered as the man of her dreams had fallen far short of her fantasy. The hero she'd searched for and thought she'd found had possessed feet of clay. Their paths had diverged days after she'd given him the news of Carlie's impending

arrival. His 'undying' love had clearly passed away at
the prospect of responsibility.

Since then, on rare occasions when her spirits were
low, she allowed herself to feel indignation on Carlie's
behalf. However, she consoled herself with the thought
that Slade Michaels was the loser, no matter how much
rodeo fame he achieved. Nor did she want Slade to pop
in and out of Carlie's life like a jack-in-the-box. She
didn't want Carlie to know what she'd learned the hard
way—that she'd only held his interest until the next opportunity for fame and fortune had beckoned.

Ben walked toward her with Percy at his side. 'What's
wrong?'

Kelly forced a smile, unaware of the frown on her
face until he'd called attention to it. 'Nothing. I was just
wool-gathering. Shall we go?'

With Carlie safely installed in the mini-van, Kelly followed Ben and Percy across town. Although darkness
hid the full details of his home, the trail of lights along
the foundation revealed a huge, two-story structure.

She parked her car in the double driveway, careful to
stay in the furthest lane. If the hospital called Ben she
didn't want to block his vehicle.

He slid open the heavy passenger door and gathered
Carlie in his arms once again, without waking her.
'She's a sound sleeper.'

'Yes.' Kelly grabbed their belongings, falling into step
beside Ben while Percy raced ahead.

Once inside she was struck by the large entryway and
the solid oak staircase, winding directly ahead. As he
navigated the steps she followed, awed by the massive
crystal chandelier and the house's opulence.

'You have a lovely home.'

'It's a little showy for my tastes.'

Obviously his ex-wife was responsible for the decor.

She wondered if he had a favorite room and, if so, what it looked like. Her speculation ran along the lines of leather-covered furniture with decorator accents in Aztec prints.

Ben carried Carlie into the first room at the top of the stairs and Kelly hurried to turn down the bed. With his burden tucked in for the night, he turned toward her. 'Your room will be next door.'

She stared at the queen-sized bed. 'If you don't mind, I'll stay here. Carlie might be scared by her new surroundings when she wakes up.'

'Suit yourself. Bathroom's down the hall to your right.' He headed for the door, then stopped. 'How's your hand?'

She ignored the ache. 'It's OK.'

He studied her face, but didn't press the point. 'There's acetaminophen and ibuprofen in the medicine cabinet. Help yourself.'

'Thanks.'

'Goodnight.' He disappeared from the room and a few minutes later she heard the distant shrill of a telephone. Shortly after, the front door opened and closed.

She rushed through a shower in a bathroom fit for a visiting dignitary, then slid under the cool sheets beside Carlie. Although tired, sleep didn't come. Instead of counting sheep, she fantasized about what it would be like to live in such a comfortable environment every day, surrounded by the possessions she'd hand-picked rather than the mismatched items commonly found in rental homes.

She'd buy antiques—solid, sturdy pieces that possessed as much character as their previous owners. She'd use bright, bold colors in her decorating scheme, not the dreary neutral shades found in nearly all her temporary residences. A few pieces by her favorite artists would grace the walls, along with her own framed pencil sketches.

As for the house itself, she wanted a bay window in her living room, at least two bathrooms and a sunny breakfast nook.

Someday, she vowed. Someday her dreams would become reality.

By the time Ben returned from the hospital, it was midnight. He parked inside the attached garage and sauntered through a short hallway to enter the kitchen, conscious of an indefinable difference in the house.

He poured himself a glass of milk. Surprised that Percy hadn't acknowledged his arrival from his pallet near the door, he glanced in the corner.

It was empty.

He drained the cup and rinsed it, before proceeding toward the stairs. Aware of his unexpected guests, he trod lightly and avoided the creaky spots on the fifth and sixth steps.

Although quiet, the entire structure hummed with a new mood. The atmosphere didn't seem as sterile and lifeless as usual. He attributed the change to his two visitors.

He sensed something else, too, but couldn't pinpoint the exact sentiment. As he neared the top of the staircase he saw Percy lying outside Kelly's and Carlie's room with his body blocking the doorway.

Suddenly alert, Percy lifted his head.

'Traitor,' Ben said affectionately, scratching the dog behind the ears. Percy had always been fiercely protective of him, but for the first time in his canine life he'd plainly enlarged his tight circle to include Carlie and Kelly.

In that instant Ben recognized the quality in the

house's ambience—peace and contentment. After Alyce and Tanya had moved out four long years ago, he'd worked hard to keep the loneliness at bay. Adopting Percy had helped, but the dog's presence hadn't totally dispelled the feeling. The festering wound of his wife's and daughter's precipitate departure had only scabbed over, not healed.

He rubbed his face. He must be more tired than he'd thought if he was diagnosing the atmosphere in his house.

The texture of rough stubble against his palms contrasted with the memory of Kelly's smooth skin and Carlie's soft body. Knowing that only a few feet separated them, his body tensed. He clenched his fists and walked towards his bedroom.

He hadn't wanted them here and he was certain Kelly had sensed the reluctance to his invitation. On some elemental level he'd suspected that the painful and passionate emotions he'd buried would surface if he spent much time with them. After two hours in her company he was proving his theory correct.

Closing the door, he flicked on the bedside lamp and stretched out on top of the spread. As he shielded his eyes with his right forearm images from the evening assaulted his mind.

The picture of Kelly in her soaked blouse caused his throat to dry. She was a lovely young woman, capable of enchanting any male with normal testosterone levels. No wonder she'd drawn Tom's interest.

As for Carlie, just thinking of the five-year-old sent a shaft of pain through his chest. She reminded him of Tanya, of everything he was missing and had already missed in his own daughter's life.

If he could have lived those days over he wouldn't have rushed into marriage with a woman so unsuited to sharing him with his patients. He'd have taken time to discover Alyce's insecurities before they'd destroyed his family.

He'd been partly to blame and he knew it. Unfortunately, he hadn't learned how to balance his career with family life and in the end his family—his daughter—had suffered.

During the years following his divorce he still hadn't acquired the skills. Living alone with a dog wasn't conducive to mastering that particular art.

He didn't *want* to feel anything for Kelly and her daughter. He refused to be trapped into the role of rescuer because he'd played that part before and had failed miserably.

He would do well to remember that.

CHAPTER FOUR

'TAKE a deep breath, Mr Bateman,' Kelly instructed the next morning. As her fifty-five-year-old patient complied she slid the large-bore needle into the prominent vein near the bend of his elbow. Her hand was stiff today and not as responsive to her commands as she'd like so she was grateful for such an easy phlebotomy.

With a practiced eye, she watched the blood flow through the tubes into the bag. 'Have you ever donated before?'

'Years ago.'

'Then you know the routine.' She stabilized the apparatus on his hairy forearm with paper-like tape.

'Yup. Since I have this polycythemia thing, Dr Shepard says you can't use this blood for anyone else. Is that right?'

'I'm afraid so,' she said. His disease was more specifically called polycythemia vera and was characterized by increased red blood cell mass. From the CBC she'd performed earlier Lewis Bateman's hematocrit was sixty per cent—much higher than the expected range of forty-five to fifty-two.

'Too bad.' He changed course. 'Did Dr Shepard say how often I had to do this?'

'Not exactly. His orders read for us to draw a unit of blood every other day until your hematocrit is less than forty-five per cent.' She studied her patient's ruddy complexion, a typical manifestation of the disease. 'It will take several therapeutic donations to reach that point.'

The corners of his mouth turned down. 'I figured as

much.' His expression perked. 'At least this isn't as bad as that bone-marrow test. I'd hate to go through that again. If givin' blood every couple of days takes care of me, I'll be a happy man.'

'That would be nice,' she agreed. Protocol demanded that she remained with the patient so she perched on a three-legged stool opposite the hospital bed to wait. A donor chair or a recliner would take up less space in their phlebotomy area but at least they weren't using a simple cot.

'Too bad there isn't a pill you can take for this, like the time I had a kidney infection. Antibiotics fixed me right up.' He waved his left hand, flashing a large turquoise ring that matched the clasp of his bolo tie and the snaps on his western-style shirt.

'Someday, perhaps.' Her curiosity aroused, she asked, 'Then your doctor hasn't prescribed any medication for you?'

Lewis shook his head. 'If this…' he motioned to the cannula in his arm '…doesn't do the trick Dr Shepard said something about taking medicine to stop the bone marrow from making extra blood. He talked about platelets, too, but I didn't catch all of that.'

So Lewis wasn't a candidate for myelosuppressive drugs. At least not yet, she silently amended. The usual procedure was, as he'd said, phlebotomy first. However, if the platelet count remained elevated or if he developed other symptoms more aggressive treatment would be required. The last polycythemia vera patient she'd encountered had shown marked improvement after several treatments with radioactive phosphorus.

Unfortunately, studies implicated this type of medical intervention with a higher risk of leukemia. With any luck, Mr Bateman would respond adequately under the less drastic protocol.

She eyed the blood bag. It was half-full. 'Do you live here in Sundance?'

'About ten miles out. Got a ranch. I'm trying to talk my two sons into coming back to help me. One lives in Portland, the other in Montana. I'll bring pictures of my grandkids next time I come. Don't get to see 'em as often as the wife and I'd like.'

Stifling a measure of guilt, Kelly made a mental note to call her mother. She'd promised to contact them after she'd settled in and she hadn't done so yet.

'Does Mrs Bateman work outside the home?'

He nodded. 'Teaches at the high school. American history. I'd promised her a vacation this summer, an Alaskan cruise, in fact, but now...' He shrugged, his voice fading. 'Looks like we won't be taking it for a while.'

'It's only the first part of June,' Kelly consoled. 'Maybe you'll be able to go in August.'

'Maybe.' He studied her. 'What about you? Got any family?'

'My parents live in Gallup. I have a daughter who turned five in May.'

He gazed intently at her left hand, as if searching for a wedding ring. 'No husband?'

Strangely enough, a mental picture of Ben appeared before her eyes and she forced the image away. 'No. No husband.'

'Pretty girl like you shouldn't have any trouble finding a fella. If you wanted one, that is.'

She felt his probing gaze. In truth, she wanted a husband and a father for Carlie, but she hadn't discovered the man worthy of filling those shoes. 'I'm waiting for the right person to come along,' she said lightly.

'Bet you get lonesome. I know I would.'

She did, but the guys she'd dated in the last year

didn't generate the sparks she wanted. After kissing a few toads, she didn't hold any hopes for finding a prince. They were already taken.

'I have five-year-old,' she said. 'I don't have time to be lonesome.'

'I see.' His mouth twisted into a knowing smile. Although he obviously saw through her white lie, he didn't comment. 'So, are you going to stay in these parts?'

'My position here is only temporary.' Actually, she wanted to stay in Sundance for the long haul. It was a friendly community with a progressive school system for Carlie. Although the town was close enough for periodic parental visits, it was also far enough away to prevent any direct interference in her daily life.

His hazel gaze sharpened. 'Move around a lot, do you?'

'About every six months,' she admitted. Her stint in Sundance would be the shortest she'd had in years. She normally asked for long-term assignments, but the time frame involved in this temporary placement suited her plans.

The unit of blood appeared full and Kelly rose. 'You're finished for today.'

'That wasn't so bad.'

'It went smoothly, didn't it?' Apologizing for the pain she was about to inflict, she grabbed one edge of the tape and tugged the strip free. It came away far more easily than she'd anticipated.

She removed the needle from his arm and applied a bandage. 'I'll give you a can of juice before you go. We don't want you passing out in the hallway.'

'That makes two of us,' he agreed, humor lighting his eyes.

While he sipped his juice Kelly disposed of the used

equipment and completed the necessary medical documentation.

'Lewis Bateman, you old rascal!' Her boss's familiar voice came from the hallway. 'I haven't seen you for so long I thought you'd retired to Arizona.' Ed Townsend strode into the cubicle to shake hands.

Lewis grinned. 'You know me. Can't stand the thought of trading my herd in for the easy life. Wouldn't know what to do with myself.'

Ed leaned against the doorframe in a relaxed pose, but the circles under his eyes and the pale hue of his face suggested he needed the support. 'What brings you to my neck of the woods?'

Lewis grimaced. 'Doctor says I've got a couple extra quarts of blood in my system. Ain't that something? I'm losing everything else under the sun—my hair, my eyesight and my teeth, even things a man can't talk about in mixed company—but I got plenty of the red stuff.'

'Tell me about it.' Ed rubbed his head, devoid of all but a few strands of dark hair, thanks to chemotherapy.

'It's hell, gettin' old, isn't it?' Lewis commented.

Ed nodded. 'That's the truth.' He tipped his head in Kelly's direction. 'How's the service?'

Lewis chortled. 'Can't complain. In fact, I'd suggest you keep this little filly. Didn't hurt me a bit,' he boasted.

'Then you don't want me to do the honors next time?'

Lewis shook his head. 'She's a darn sight prettier to look at than you.'

Ed smiled, clearly enjoying the friendly banter. 'I can't argue with you.'

'If you two don't stop that,' Kelly scolded without rancor, 'I'm going to tell your wives about your roving eyes.'

Lewis brushed aside her rebuke. 'I'm old, not dead.'

Kelly smiled. 'In that case, if you're feeling OK, Mr Bateman—no dizziness or nausea—you're free to go.'

Lewis grabbed his Stetson off the edge of the bed as he rose. 'See ya in a few days.' He accompanied Ed outside the cubicle, then turned towards her as she followed them into the hallway. 'I've got a couple of new colts, in case your daughter's interested in seein' 'em.'

'She'd love to. Thank you.'

'Come anytime.' He planted his hat on his head, shook hands with Ed, then ambled away.

'Is Dee around?' Ed asked. 'I want to talk to the two of you. I have a few things to discuss.'

Concerned over his growing pallor, she nodded. 'I'll get her. We'll meet you in your office.'

Offering no argument, he disappeared into the room designated as his.

After relaying the request to Dee, the two entered his private sanctum a few minutes later and sat in the chairs near his desk. 'What's up?' Dee asked.

Ed's attention landed on Kelly. 'Before I get started, how's your hand?'

Embarrassed by his attention, her face warmed. 'It's a little stiff and sore but nothing I can't live with.'

Apparently satisfied by her remark, he said, 'Ben called me this morning. He'd asked if I'd make sure you didn't ruin his handiwork.'

Kelly didn't know if she should be flattered or aggravated. She chose the latter. She didn't need Ben looking out for her and intended to tell him so at her first opportunity. 'I know my limitations.'

Dee glanced at her. 'Handiwork? I thought you had a minor cut. What did he do?'

'He put a few stitches in my palm.'

'Stitches? You didn't tell me this earlier.'

'It's no big deal.'

'When did this happen?' Dee sounded incredulous.

'Last night.' Conscious of her boss's as-yet-undisclosed agenda, she murmured, 'I'll tell you about it later.'

'Just be careful,' Ed admonished. 'I asked you both here because I have a problem.' The dismay on their faces must have been obvious because he chuckled. 'Don't look at me like that. It isn't what you're thinking.'

Kelly exchanged a relieved glance with Dee.

'As you know, I've been on chemotherapy since they removed part of my colon and several lymph nodes. Unfortunately, by the time I start to feel better after one session it's time for another.

'I'm having a hard time, staying on top of things, because I can't concentrate very well. My memory isn't as sharp as it was either. So, between my limitations and frequent absences, I can't handle the latest project I've been given. I hate to dump it on you, but I don't have a choice.'

'No problem,' Dee declared. 'The two of us can surely steal a few minutes away from the bench. We'll manage.'

'You may change your mind when I tell you what's involved,' Ed warned. 'As you've probably heard, the hospital is running over budget. The accounting folks are in a panic. Every department has been instructed to tighten its belt and cut expenses by at least twenty per cent over the next ninety days. I need you gals to find and eliminate that twenty per cent, without compromising services or patient care.'

Dee whistled. 'Sounds like *Mission Impossible* to me.'

'It won't be easy,' he agreed.

Dee held up her hands. 'I take back what I said earlier. Count me out. I can't find a seventy-five cent error in my last bank statement, and you want me to look for thousands of dollars?' She shook her head for emphasis. 'I abdicate responsibility to my younger and much brighter colleague.'

Ed's questioning gaze fell on Kelly. Feeling the pressure of the spotlight, she shrugged, unable to refuse. At the same time she wasn't enthusiastic about this project. The assignment filled her with more misgivings than confidence. 'I'll do my best but, remember, I'm new—'

'Then it's settled,' he said, sounding relieved. 'Dr Shepard has agreed to review our test menu and see if the doctors can agree on cutting any rarely requested in-house procedures. If you need any advice, talk to him.'

Kelly's heart rate accelerated at the mention of Ben's name. Fate seemed determined to throw them together at every turn. Her stomach rebelled, but she didn't know whether it was due to excitement or tension over the prospect of working with him.

'Vanessa Osbourne in Purchasing will send the purchasing print-outs for the last quarter over later this afternoon,' Ed finished before he rose. 'Now, if you don't mind, I'm going home.'

Kelly and Dee made a hasty exit. Back in the lab Dee shook her head. 'What a job! We went through this about a year ago and I thought we'd pared down everything possible then. If there's any fat to trim, it isn't in this department.'

Privately, Kelly agreed. She had a few ideas for economizing, but the savings realized from those changes wouldn't add up to the required twenty per cent. 'We'll look at the print-outs together. Maybe something will stand out.'

Dee snorted. 'Don't hold your breath. I mean this in the nicest possible way, but I'm glad you're on the task force instead of me. This is one of those do-or-die jobs and, quite frankly, I don't need or want the extra pressure.'

Neither do I, Kelly thought. Yet if success would give her an 'in' when it came time to hire permanent staff, she wouldn't fail. After all, she had more at stake than presenting a good recommendation to her employers at TLC, Inc.

Her daughter's fate lay in the balance.

'Mommy? Can we stay at Dr Ben's tonight?' Carlie's expression matched her pleading tone. 'His bed was really, really, comf'table.'

Driving through town, Kelly agreed. The cushiony softness of his mattress had given her the most restful night she'd experienced in ages. Over the years she'd slept in many beds which had been either too hard or too soft. Rarely had she found one that was just right. How ironic to discover the perfect accommodations at Ben Shepard's house.

She couldn't help but wonder what *his* bed was like. It would have to be large enough to accommodate his height and still have room for the person he'd choose to share it with.

The thought of being that individual sent a delightful shudder rippling through her. She tightened her grip on the steering-wheel as her imagination brought a smile to her lips.

Carlie sneezed, bringing Kelly out of her daydream. Her mind raced to pick up the thread of their conversation. 'The bed was great, wasn't it?' she agreed. 'But we're staying at our place. The repairman fixed the bathtub today.' *I hope*, she finished silently.

'Oh.' Carlie stared at the passing scenery on their way home. 'Then could we just drop by for a visit? I promised Percy I'd bring him a doggy biscuit.'

'I'm afraid not. We don't have any dog biscuits with us.'

'But, Mommy, didn't you say we should always honor our promises?'

The little scamp was too smart for her own good. 'Yes, but—'

'Well, I promised Percy a treat and I wanna give him one.' Carlie folded her arms over her chest. Lowering her chin, she settled her mouth into a familiar pout.

Kelly gave in to the inevitable. Her hand was throbbing from doing too much too soon, and she didn't want to fight over a bone.

'And you will. However, we have to wait until the next time we go to the store. It may be a day or two,' she warned.

Carlie screwed up her face, considering the compromise. 'Do you think Percy will mind if he has to wait an extra day?'

'Once you give him his treat he'll forget how long he had to wait,' Kelly reassured her, turning onto the concrete driveway which led to the detached single-car garage.

A few minutes later Carlie bounded inside the house. Kelly followed more sedately, juggling her purse, an unwieldy folder bulging with computer print-outs and her lunch box.

Carlie beckoned her from the bathroom doorway. 'Come and see, Mommy.'

Kelly found a gleaming set of chrome fixtures. She turned the knob, pleased to see the water disappear down the drain with ease.

'Looks like we can't stay at Dr Ben's house,' Carlie mourned.

'We wouldn't even if no one repaired the tub today,'

Kelly told her daughter kindly. 'We couldn't impose on him again.'

'He wouldn't mind.' Carlie sounded certain.

Kelly begged to differ, but kept her opinion to herself. She attempted to divert Carlie's attention as they returned to the kitchen. 'Why don't we call Grandma and Grandpa? I'll bet they're anxious to talk to you.'

'OK.' Under Kelly's supervision, Carlie punched the long sequence of numbers. She listened intently before her face broke into a huge smile. 'Hi, Grandma.'

After a short pause, Carlie spoke. 'One of the boys is always mean to me, but the girls are OK. None of them can count as good as I can, though.'

From Carlie's reply Kelly knew her mother had asked about her new friends. She motioned for her to hand over the receiver. 'Hi, Mom,' she said.

'We were wondering when you'd call,' Virginia Evers chided. 'Your father was getting worried.'

Kelly refused to accept the guilt her parents tried to load on her shoulders. However, it was easier said than done. 'You know we need time to settle into a new place.'

'All the more reason to find a steady job.' Winston Evers's voice entered the conversation.

Kelly gritted her teeth. If only they didn't own an extension. It was difficult enough, dealing with them one at a time. Together it was nearly impossible.

'I have a steady job,' she reminded them. 'The location just varies.'

'How's Carlie adjusting?' Virginia asked. 'What's this about a boy being mean to her?'

Kelly crossed her fingers. 'A minor squabble. You know how kids are. But she's doing great. Honest.'

'School will start in two and a half months. Have you figured out what you're going to do?' Winston pressed.

Kelly closed her eyes and sagged into a chair. 'Not yet, Dad. But I will.'

'You really ought to make plans. I talked to the principal the other day about adding Carlie to their roster. The sooner they know she'll be coming the better.'

'Dad, I have plenty of time,' Kelly said, holding onto her temper although she could feel her body tense. 'I'm hoping to find a permanent position before the fall session begins.'

'If not, you'll let Carlie live with us. Right?'

Kelly sighed. Over the past year her parents had brought up the subject with frightening regularity. Their initial subtle hints had changed into strong suggestions, although they'd been careful not to make any demands. In the aftermath of one intense badgering session Kelly had agreed to consider their proposal. Although she considered their offer as another option, her parents acted as if it were her only alternative. Perhaps it was.

She hated the thought of separating herself from her daughter, and she especially hated the thought of giving her parents control over a part of her life. It had taken every ounce of her courage to break out of their stifling embrace years ago. The thought of re-entering the situation was untenable.

And yet Carlie's needs came first.

She lowered her voice. 'If it comes to that Carlie can live with you. I'm hoping it won't.'

'Of course.' Thanks to the phone company's excellent fiberoptics, her father's patronizing tone was obvious. 'We just want what's best for Carlie.'

Kelly gritted her teeth. 'So do I. In the meantime, don't redecorate my old room yet.'

Silence came over the line. Anger began to build at the notion of her parents' actions. 'You haven't, have you?'

'Now, Kelly. All I've done is given it a fresh coat of paint, found new curtains and a matching bedspread.'

Kelly counted to ten in French, before answering. 'Don't do anything else. As I said earlier, nothing is definite.' Even if she had to move heaven and earth, she wouldn't give up her daughter to her well-meaning parents, even temporarily.

'We understand. Even if she doesn't live with us,' Virginia soothed, 'the room will be special for your visits.'

Knowing her arguments would be disregarded, Kelly didn't offer any. 'I'd better go. We haven't had supper yet. I'll call you again.'

'Put Carlie back on,' Winston said. 'I want to say goodbye.'

As soon as Carlie held out the receiver Kelly went to the bathroom where she splashed water on her face and willed herself to be calm. Her parents meant well, but they never understood her need to be independent. Even her mother hadn't been her ally. Virginia Evers didn't make a move without her husband's blessing.

That wasn't the sort of marriage Kelly wanted or dreamed of having. She wanted a partnership, not a dictatorship. She had a brain and intended to use it. Furthermore, she planned on raising her daughter with a different set of expectations than she'd been given. Carlie wouldn't be the doormat Kelly had been for the first twenty-some years of her life.

The pain in her hand intensified, pulling her out of her reverie. She glanced down, surprised to see her fingers clenched in a loose fist. No wonder her injury ached.

She retrieved the small bottle of extra-strength pain relievers from the medicine cabinet and gulped down the last two. After supper she'd run to the store for more while Carlie picked out a treat for Percy. At least her daughter's worries would be over.

If only Kelly's could disappear as easily.

Ben stood on the porch, berating himself for his weakness. He could have easily checked on the water situation via telephone, rather than by putting in a personal appearance. Much as he hated to admit it, something compelled him to drive by and see for himself that everything was in order.

Once he did so he'd be able to shake Kelly and her daughter out of his thoughts. They'd appeared in his mind's eye more times throughout the day than he cared to count, and although he'd tried to relegate them to a distant memory he couldn't.

In any event, he'd ask if the plumbing situation was in order, then leave. It would take five minutes of his time, no more. His responsibilities to them would end and his life would return to normal.

Carlie answered his knock. Her face lit up as soon as she saw him and she welcomed him inside. 'Where's Percy?'

So much for her excitement over him, he thought wryly. 'He's in the truck, waiting for me.'

Kelly stood behind her pint-sized replica. 'Please come in.'

He shook his head, glad for his prepared excuse. 'I can't. I only dropped by to make sure someone repaired the faucet and drain today.'

She smiled. 'Everything's in tip-top shape.'

'Good. How's your hand?'

Kelly stared at his chin rather than his eyes. 'Sore. I tried not to overuse it, but it's amazing how difficult it is to function when you're used to ten fingers instead of five.'

He tallied a point for honesty. 'Watch for any signs of redness, puffiness or infection.'

'I will.'

'Wanna stay for supper, Dr Ben?' Carlie asked.

He hesitated. Something did smell good. Maybe it was one of her infamous tuna casseroles.

'Macaroni and cheese,' Carlie informed him. 'My mommy makes the bestest there is. Do you like macaroni and cheese?'

'Yes, I do.' For some strange reason he found himself actually considering their invitation. He hadn't eaten the dish in ages—it had been Tanya's favorite.

'You're welcome to join us,' Kelly offered. 'I have plenty for everyone.'

'We've even got a special bone for Percy,' Carlie interrupted. 'He won't go hungry neither.'

He smiled at her ungrammatical sentence, knowing he should refuse. Although his taste buds clamored for satisfaction, spending time with these two would be emotional suicide.

Carlie's pleading expression wasn't helping. The raw hope on her face chipped away at his resolve. Her eyes reminded him so much of his own daughter's when she'd begged him to attend her pre-school Christmas program. He'd disappointed his own child in so many ways—he didn't have the heart to disappoint this one too.

He would, though. His track record proved it. Life would be better for all of them—him especially—if he maintained an aloof distance, no matter how much he wanted to do otherwise.

'I can't. Have a nice evening.' He strode toward his vehicle before he changed his mind.

Kelly watched his retreat without a word, noticing the way his shirt stretched across his back and his khaki trousers molded his legs and hips. She'd been touched by his visit and his concern. Although she didn't show her excitement over his presence like Carlie did, she'd felt it in her heart.

And like Carlie, his refusal had deflated her joy, leaving massive disappointment in its wake.

Carlie stared up at Kelly. 'Why did he leave, Mommy? I thought he wanted to stay.'

'I thought so too,' Kelly replied softly. She'd seen the yearning on his face and had been certain that he'd accept their invitation. In the blink of an eye, however, his familiar stony-faced expression had settled into place.

It was almost as if he were afraid to accept. Did he think that she planned to trap him into an unwanted and undesirable relationship with a macaroni-and-cheese casserole?

Or was he afraid of the relationship itself? Some men avoided commitment like the plague—Carlie's father was one of them. And yet Ben didn't exhibit the same self-centeredness she'd eventually seen in Slade. Then again, maybe she was reading more into the situation than necessary.

'He's a busy man with a lot of responsibilities,' she told Carlie, leading her to the kitchen table. 'I'm sure he had another appointment. Now, let's eat.'

Carlie's mouth drooped at the corners. 'He forgot Percy's treat.'

'We'll drop it by tomorrow,' Kelly promised.

'Can't we take it by after supper?'

Kelly was ready to refuse, but the more she considered the suggestion the better it sounded. Percy would get his bone and she would get her answers.

CHAPTER FIVE

DEE dropped the receiver in its cradle. 'ER has a case of rattlesnake bite and needs lab work. Are you available?'

Kelly nodded as she wiped the oil from the last slide. 'Yes. I just finished.'

'Good. I'd volunteer, but Dr Martin is waiting for this digoxin result.'

Kelly rose to wash her hands and grab her tray. She arrived in the ER a few minutes later, catching a glimpse of Ben and the two nurses before they disappeared into the trauma room with a young man in his early twenties.

Three weeks had elapsed since she'd last seen Ben on her doorstep, three weeks since she'd felt his blatant rejection.

During the subsequent days she'd expected some sort of acknowledgement for the rawhide chew they'd left on Ben's doorstep. Carlie had too. Her daughter had stayed close to the telephone and doorbell until two weeks had passed. By then she'd accepted the obvious.

Thanks to Ben's nurse-practitioner, who'd removed Kelly's stitches, she'd learned that he'd covered the satellite clinics sponsored by the Sundance Community Hospital for seven of those days to help out a colleague.

She could understand how busy he must have been with his regular patients upon his return. Even so, a brief message to a child wouldn't have come amiss. Most people could work a thirty-second conversation into their schedule.

She'd wanted to berate him with every bit of her being

for his rudeness to Carlie. In the end, however, good sense had overruled her temper. She'd vowed to take an aloof approach if their paths ever crossed outside the hospital. So far they hadn't.

Waiting for his instructions, she stood inside the trauma room doorway and prepared her supplies. With the patient's buddy—a young man also in his twenties— beside her, the scene unfolded and she watched like a spectator at a motion picture.

'Start an IV with a large-bore needle for the antivenin,' Ben ordered, standing over the gurney bearing his supine patient. 'What's your name?'

'Gil Stephens.'

One of the nurses ripped open a sterile infusion set. 'How many lines?'

'Two. Run the antivenin through one and keep the other open in case we need it.' He studied Gil's leg. Although Kelly couldn't see Gil's face, someone had cut off the leg of his jeans, giving her an excellent view of his injury. The site on his shin was swollen and the skin discolored. Kelly winced in sympathy.

'Any numbness or tingling in your toes?'

'Some.'

'How long ago did this happen?' Ben asked, his attention riveted to the wound.

Gil's friend stepped closer to the gurney. 'Fifteen, twenty minutes, tops. We were setting up camp on Sundance Mountain.'

'At least you weren't too far away,' someone commented.

Gil's chuckle sounded weak. 'Even so, I think we flew here. John didn't pay attention to speed zones.'

'What happened?' Ben asked.

'We kept a close eye out for snakes on our trail, but never saw any,' Gil explained. His voice quivered and he cleared his throat a few times. 'Being so close to a holiday, we saw more campers than wildlife. Anyway, we started to hike in a remote area. The next thing I knew I felt this stinging pain just below my knee. I looked and saw a rattler.'

John wore a worried expression. 'Should I have sucked out the poison or applied a tourniquet? I've heard different stories about what to do.'

Ben continued his probing assessment. 'Unfortunately, authorities don't agree on the best first aid. Some discourage it unless you're a long distance from medical treatment—more than forty minutes away. Others suggest giving immediate attention. For your future reference, if you decide to intervene, do it within the first fifteen minutes.'

'Man, I hope this won't happen again,' John said.

'Since we were so close,' Ben added, 'you made the right choice to bring him here rather than waste time in the field.'

John's shoulders slumped in obvious relief.

Ben glanced in Kelly's direction. 'I want a CBC, coagulation tests, blood typing, electrolytes, BUN and creatinine right away. And a UA.'

Kelly moved to the bedside and began her task of drawing the necessary tubes of blood while Ben listened to Gil's heart rate. 'Did you drink anything alcoholic or caffeinated?'

Gil shook his head, but John spoke. 'Would it matter?'

Ben flung the stethoscope around his neck. 'Stimulants and alcohol speed the venom's absorption. We're going to give you a tetanus injection and antibiotics as snakes have a lot of bacteria in their mouths. How's the pain?'

Gil shuddered. 'It hurts, that's for sure.'

'You can have a few acetaminophen. We'll observe

you for at least twenty-four hours so if you need to notify any family…'

'My folks.'

John stepped forward. 'I'll call 'em. Don't worry
about a thing. You're gonna be fine.'

Kelly labelled her samples and hurried out of the
room. Ben's requests would take a while to complete.
In the meantime, the nursing staff would periodically
assess Gil's condition and perform hypersensitivity tests
to the antivenin. If he showed a reaction to the horse
serum it contained, Dr Shepard would adjust his treatment plan accordingly.

'Looks like we'll be busy with this one for a while,'
she told Dee as she placed the appropriate specimens in
the centrifuge.

'That bad?' Dee asked.

'It's serious, but Dr Shepard didn't act like this was
a critical case. Then again, he's a hard man to second-
guess.'

'If he's anxious for results they'll call in a few
minutes,' Dee predicted. 'The bigger the rush the less
time they give us to get the answers.'

Ten minutes later the telephone rang.

'Any results yet?' Cheryl, the ER supervisor, asked.

Kelly recited her CBC findings, noting the decreased
hemoglobin and platelet levels. The coag. studies were
increased, showing that the venom was affecting Gil's
normal clotting mechanism. Ben would calculate the
dosage of antivenin to be administered based on her results.

By the time she'd completed her share of Gil
Stephens's tests several outpatients had arrived, including Lewis Bateman.

'Let the others go first,' he told her. 'No sense in them
waitin' on account of me.'

Kelly smiled at the grizzled rancher. 'You don't mind?'

'Not a bit. My wife's shopping, anyway, so I figure I've got at least two hours to waste.' He grinned.

'I promise not to keep you the whole time,' she said.

Her first patient was Emma Whistler, a young woman in her mid-twenties. The tests recorded on her order form indicated an infertility problem, which Emma confirmed as she pushed up her sleeve.

'We've been trying to have a baby for three years now,' Emma confessed. 'Dr Powell is sending me to a specialist in Rapid City, but he wants the blood work done before my appointment next week.'

'I'll make a note to forward copies to both physicians,' Kelly stated. 'We should have the results of the hormone levels in a few days.'

'Good,' Emma declared. 'I'm anxious to know what's wrong so we can start our family. My sister's already had two children and she's younger than I am. Do you suppose that being on the Pill for so many years has done something?'

Kelly withdrew the needle from Emma's arm and applied a bandage. 'I really can't say,' she said. 'Have you discussed this with your doctor?'

'I mentioned it, but all he told me was not to worry. It's easy for him to say when his body isn't the one not functioning the way God intended.'

'Worrying doesn't change anything,' Kelly commented. 'If I were you I'd follow his advice.' She ushered her to the door. 'Good luck.'

'Thanks.'

Emma left and Cade Rogers came in. A distinguished man in his early forties, he wore a dark business suit and black wing-tipped shoes. His paperwork indicated pre-surgical testing and Kelly wondered what type of surgery such a healthy-looking man needed.

'How are you today?' she asked cheerfully, trying to break the cold mood surrounding him.

'Fine.' He rolled up the long sleeve of his white shirt with precise motions. 'How long will this take?'

She swiped alcohol across his skin, inserted the needle and popped on the first tube. Blood spurted into the vial. 'Just another minute or two.'

'Good. I'm supposed to be at the courthouse in twenty minutes.'

'You must be a lawyer.'

'A judge, actually.'

She wondered if she should apologize for her ignorance, but before she voiced anything he continued.

'To be honest, after being involved in malpractice suits, the thought of putting my life in someone's hands is frightening,' he admitted.

He was obviously hiding his fear behind his abrupt manner. At the same time Kelly's sympathies fell on the surgeon and nursing staff. They couldn't afford to make any mistakes, no matter how minor.

He sighed. 'But I've been assured that a hernia repair is no big deal. I should be in and out of the hospital on the same day. I'd better be too. I don't have time to be incapacitated for days.'

Kelly withheld comment. Even if the surgeon released him on schedule, it would be some time before he was fit to work. She hoped his doctor explained this thoroughly beforehand or else he would have one unhappy patient.

After he left she called Lewis's name. He rose, carrying his Stetson. 'Hope you weren't bored, waiting for me.'

'Nope.' He made himself comfortable on the bed. 'I

get a kick out of watchin' folks. Take that Judge Rogers. He's got an over-inflated view of himself, if you ask me. Then again, I don't think highly of many lawyers anyways. Too greedy. Always lookin' for ways to make a buck out of someone else's misery.'

He crossed his legs at the ankles. 'Enough of that nonsense. What's happenin' with your little one?'

Kelly grinned. Except for a few recent bed-wetting accidents, everything was fine. 'The usual. Her energy level is phenomenal.'

He nodded. 'My wife, Betty Jean, always wished we could bottle our kids' energy and sell it. We'd have been rich.'

Kelly laughed. 'I agree. By the way, we're still planning on visiting your colts this weekend.'

'That'll be great. They're a pure joy to watch.' His eyes took on a far-away look. 'Betty Jean and I sit on the porch after supper and watch 'em run around in the pasture. Nippin' at each other and playin' just like kids.'

'Carlie will love it.'

Lewis pointed towards the north side of the room. 'I noticed the sky was looking mighty blue when we came to town. Forecast says seventy per cent chance of rain tonight, along with high winds. I'm guessing it'll hit us by early evening.'

'What makes you say that?' She grinned. 'A trick knee?'

'Don't laugh, young lady,' he said good-naturedly. 'It's my shoulder. Ever since I broke my collar-bone a few years ago I can always tell when we're in for a storm. The way it aches today we're in for a doosie.'

'I hope not,' she said fervently. While she didn't mind the rain, she hated the thunder and lightning that often accompanied it. She didn't have a particular reason for her dislike, but she had it nonetheless.

He shrugged, clearly unabashed with his gift. 'The old-timers can predict the weather better than those TV weathermen and their high-powered satellites. A rancher learns to read the signs if he plans on his herd surviving.'

'My dad says the same thing.' Her father had always understood Mother Nature far better than he had his own daughter.

Kelly eyed the unit of blood and deemed it full. 'Looks like I've got today's quota. Once you drink your juice you're free to leave.'

Lewis drained the cup in one long gulp, then smacked his lips. 'Betty Jean and I will be watching for you on Saturday.'

'Fair enough.'

'I wouldn't run around town, tonight,' he advised. 'It won't be fit for man nor beast.'

'Thanks for the warning.' Convinced by Lewis's sincerity, Kelly decided to stop at the grocery store as soon as she picked up Carlie from the day-care center. Although she'd planned her excursion for after dinner she wanted to be safe at home before the storm came.

By the time they arrived at the store a large bank of menacing dark clouds was advancing from the northwest, turning the air cool. Occasional sheets of lightning ripped across the sky and a few flashes snaked down to earth in a jagged line. She hurried Carlie inside and grabbed the nearest cart to hold their purchases.

'I wanna push.'

Knowing Carlie couldn't see over the handle, Kelly tried to dissuade her. 'How about a ride?'

Carlie shook her head and her face exhibited a familiar stubbornness. 'I wanna push,' she repeated.

Trying to convince her otherwise would have taken more time than it was worth. Kelly capitulated. 'You push while I guide. But we have to hurry. We want to get home before it storms.'

They'd turned down the first aisle and Kelly's gaze was drawn to the tall man selecting apples from the fruit display in the center. Before she could divert Carlie's attention the child spotted him as well.

'It's Dr Ben!' Carlie abandoned the cart to rush ahead before Kelly could protest.

Why did the man have to be so blasted tall? she thought unreasonably. Anyone would have to be blind not to notice him, towering over everyone else, and Carlie was certainly not blind. In fact, very little seemed to escape her daughter's inquisitive eyes.

Wishing she could forego this meeting, Kelly slowed her steps to grab a head of lettuce, a package of carrots and a bag of oranges along the way. She'd give him a polite greeting—not that he deserved one—before hurrying on to the next row of goods. An imp of mischief made her take her time approaching, although she was close enough to hear their conversation.

'Did Percy like his bone?' Carlie asked, staring into Ben's face with something akin to adoration.

'Yes, he did. Thanks for thinking of him. Is your mother around?'

'She's coming. Over there.'

He glanced in the direction Carlie had indicated, his expression inscrutable.

'Do you think it might rain?' Carlie asked.

'Yes, I do.'

'My mommy hates storms.'

'Oh, she does,' he said politely.

Certain she'd given them enough time together, Kelly wheeled her cart next to his. 'Let's go, sweetie.'

'But I wanna visit with Dr Ben. He hasn't said how Percy is.'

Ben looked down on Carlie. 'He's fine.'

'Will you bring him over to play again some time?'

'We'll see.'

Her gaze fixed on Ben's face, Carlie tilted her head slightly, as if trying to ease the tension in her neck. 'Is that a yes or a no?'

'It means that I don't know. It depends on my schedule,' he said.

'Oh.'

Before she could pose another question he continued, 'Meanwhile, you'd better stay with your mom. This is a big store and you might get lost.'

'Can I walk with you?'

Indecision warred on his face before he shook his head. 'Better not. I'm in a hurry.'

'That's OK. So's Mommy.'

Kelly had to admit one thing—Carlie exhibited enough persistence for both of them. 'Sorry, honey, but I want you near me.'

She gave him a pointed stare, mentally telegraphing her own message that she recognized his dislike for their company. 'Now, it's time to get the rest of our groceries,' she said, nudging Carlie forward. 'If you'll excuse us?'

Without waiting for Ben's reply, she moved past him at a faster pace than when she'd approached.

Carlie's feet dragged as they travelled down the aisle. The longing glances she directed toward Ben over her tiny shoulder didn't escape Kelly's notice. Righteous anger filled her soul.

Carlie had suffered enough rejection in her life from her father—she didn't need any from Ben Shepard. Once again she berated herself for her poor character judgement. To think she'd fantasized about Ben in her weak moments. Well, no more.

She tossed a box of crackers into the cart with enough force to create crumbs. Inhaling a deep breath to relax, she studied her daughter.

Carlie plodded along, dejected. 'Why doesn't he like us, Mommy?'

Kelly sighed. She'd asked herself the same question and hadn't thought of a suitable answer. 'I don't know, sweetie. I honestly don't know.'

Perhaps she could get some insight from Tom, but she hated the idea of calling him. It would seem like she was whining. Tom couldn't change the situation anyway. She and Ben were in the category of people whose personalities, for some unknown reason, didn't mesh.

Without encouragement, and over time, Carlie's case of hero-worship would die a natural death. Like her mother, she would learn that true heroes were in short supply.

A clap of thunder reverberated through the house like a pistol shot, breaking Ben's concentration. The white billiard ball struck a glancing blow against the number eleven stripe. It careened to the left rather than into the side pocket.

Percy rubbed against Ben's right leg and whimpered.

Ben scratched the dog's ears. 'You don't like the thunder either, do you?'

Percy whimpered again.

Unbidden, Carlie's comment about Kelly hating storms came to mind. Although he didn't want to worry about their welfare, he found himself doing so.

This was all Tom's fault, he thought. If his brother hadn't given Kelly the key, and hadn't asked him to look after her and her daughter, Ben could dismiss them as easily as he did most people. If Tom ever found time to return his phone calls he intended to tell him once and for all to find someone else to carry out his rescue missions.

Billiards forgotten, Ben sank onto a nearby easy chair. Percy laid his head on Ben's knee and he absent-mindedly stroked the Dalmatian's forehead. Instantly, a mental picture of a stuffed Perdita formed. An image of its small owner followed.

'Why doesn't he like us, Mommy?' Carlie's plaintive note as he'd overheard her question had been like a knife thrust in his belly. In that split second he'd heard her regard for him shatter into a thousand pieces.

It was ridiculous to wish it could be otherwise—he had no one to blame but himself. How could he explain to a five-year-old that the problem didn't lie with her or her mother, but came from within himself?

It wasn't fair to make Carlie suffer because of his own pain. He had to deal with this situation. Ignoring it wouldn't make it go away, especially if the youngster became his niece. In fact, a measure of envy now replaced his earlier reservations concerning Tom's engagement.

Lightning flashed and another clap of thunder followed in its wake. The lights flickered, then went out.

Having expected to lose electricity with the advent of the storm, Ben had placed a flashlight on the nearby coffee-table. He groped for it until he located the sleek cylinder and pressed the switch. A beam of light parted the darkness and he made his way to the window, without stumbling.

Everything was pitch black. Gusts of rain beat against the windows in a rapid staccato and the wind howled as it whipped around the buildings. Before long a faint glow appeared in the house across the street as his neighbors located flashlights and candles.

His thoughts raced to another house, this one across

town. Would Kelly find the stash of emergency supplies and matches in the bottom kitchen drawer? What if she didn't?

Muttering an oath at his over-active conscience, he strode toward the telephone and grabbed the receiver. Static on the line rendered the phone virtually inoperable.

Without stopping to reconsider, he snapped his fingers at Percy. 'Let's go, boy.'

As if knowing their destination, Percy bounded through the house to the garage door. He arrived moments before Ben and stood patiently with his nose inches away from the doorknob.

Ben scratched Percy's ears affectionately. 'In a hurry, are you?'

The Dalmatian woofed in reply.

Ben collected a yellow slicker hanging on the peg behind the door, a second flashlight and extra batteries. A minute later he flung open the truck door. Percy jumped inside while he stowed his supplies on the seat.

Focusing his attention on the wet street stretching ahead of him, he mentally prepared for a chilly reception and practiced an apology.

'Mommy, why aren't the lights coming back on? I'm scared.' In the flickering candle's glow Carlie's fear showed plainly. Her lower lip quivered as much as the Old Maid cards in her hand did. She winced and covered her ears with each clap of thunder and bolt of lightning.

Kelly wasn't fond of the situation either, but Carlie wouldn't relax if she thought the weather frightened her own mother. 'It'll be all right. We're safe and snug and having a good time. Now, it's your turn to pick.'

Thunder boomed and the picture window a few feet

away shook from the force. Carlie dropped her cards and flung herself into Kelly's arms.

'It's OK, sweetie,' Kelly soothed, stroking Carlie's baby-fine hair. 'It's only noise. It won't hurt us. Now, let's finish our game.'

Carlie kept her face buried in Kelly's chest. 'Don't want to.'

'OK. Then I guess I win.' Knowing how Carlie hated to lose, Kelly hoped to revive her competitive spirit.

After a momentary hesitation Carlie pulled out of Kelly's embrace, gathered her cards and repositioned them in her hand. 'My turn to pick,' she said.

After the next few exchanges the Old Maid card remained in Kelly's hand. 'I win!' Carlie crowed as she scooped the pairs into a pile.

Kelly grinned. 'Yes, you did. It's eight o'clock. Off to bed.'

Lightning crackled and the thunder sounded like a bomb blast. Carlie held her hands over her ears and her voice was tearful. 'Mommy! Do I have to go now?'

Kelly crouched down and hugged her. 'Yes. If you don't go to sleep you'll be too tired to play with your friends tomorrow.'

'But I can't sleep with the lightnin' shinin' in my eyes.'

'You can if you close them.'

'And the thunder's too loud for my ears.'

Kelly hid her smile at Carlie's excuses. Once she fell asleep nothing could wake her. 'It will stop soon. The weatherman said so.'

'Will you lay by me?'

Kelly could hardly refuse her child's request, not when she clearly needed the comfort of another person. 'Until it stops raining.' Or until you fall asleep, she silently amended.

The worry on the little girl's face faded.

Thinking of Carlie's recent accidents, Kelly asked, 'Did you take care of your bathroom business?'

Carlie nodded and Kelly rose.

'Then hop in bed. Take the flashlight,' she added as an afterthought.

A yellowish beam danced along the floor and walls as Carlie went on her way.

Out of habit, Kelly rechecked the lock on the door. Intending to return to the living room and her budget print-outs after Carlie fell asleep, she left the fat blueberry-scented candle burning on the corner end table.

She picked up one of the tapers and cupped her hand around the burning wick as she followed Carlie. Once in the bedroom she snuffed out the tiny orange flame and crawled under the lightweight quilt. The smell of smoke lingered in the darkness.

Carlie snuggled against her. 'I wish the 'lectricity would come on. I don't have a night-light.' Her voice was wistful.

'If you need to go anywhere you can use the flashlight.'

Carlie sat up to give her a kiss. In the darkness her lips landed on Kelly's chin and the child giggled. 'G'night, Mommy.'

'Goodnight, sweets.'

Rain pelted the roof and thunder interrupted the wind's mournful tune. Carlie burrowed herself against Kelly's side in short order. Her small voice seemed out of place amid the cacophony of the storm.

'I hope Percy is warm. Do you suppose Dr Ben lets him sleep inside? He did when we stayed there.'

'I'm sure he does.'

Carlie sighed. 'I hope Dr Ben lets me play with Percy some time.'

Kelly tensed. It had taken two games of Chutes and Ladders to snap Carlie out of her doldrums after their trip to the store. She didn't want her to become upset again by thinking about the Dalmatian or Ben Shepard.

'Let's not worry about it now,' she said, keeping her voice even. Although the chances of that happening were slim to none, she didn't want to shatter all of Carlie's hopes. With any luck, the Batemans' new colts would replace the Dalmatian in her thoughts. If not, she could always dognap Percy for an afternoon.

'When can I have my own real, live Dalmatian?'

The familiar question brought forth the standard response. 'When we have a house of our very own.'

'When will that be?'

Another familiar question. 'Soon, honey. Soon.' I hope. 'Now go to sleep. Sweet dreams.'

Carlie rolled over to face the wall. Long moments passed. Lulled by the child's slow and steady breathing, Kelly's eyes drifted closed. Just as she groggily reminded herself to wake Carlie in a few hours to use the bathroom something struck the front door.

Kelly's eyelids flew open, uncertain if the storm had created the noise or if she'd dreamed it.

The pounding came again. Someone was outside.

She eased out from under the thin blanket and reached for the flashlight, careful not to disturb her sleepy daughter. Once she entered the hallway she pressed the switch and trained the beam directly ahead.

The doorknob rattled, followed by a woof. Hardly believing her instinct that it was Ben, paying a visit, she peeked through the security hole. The hood of the man's yellow slicker cast shadows on his face which obliterated his identity, but as he turned to gaze into the distance the glow from a torch revealed Ben's profile.

Kelly sagged against the door. What was he doing

here? What could he possibly want? He'd made it plain that he didn't want to associate with them so why did he always appear like a bad penny?

'Kelly!' he called, hammering the door with his fist.

She straightened. Squaring her shoulders and bracing herself against the cold, she greeted him face to face.

'If you're checking on us, don't bother,' she said in her most frosty tone. 'You may think that I don't have enough sense to come in out of the rain but, as you can see, I'm dry and you're not.'

He brushed past her without any invitation, showering her bare legs with cold droplets of water. Percy followed him inside. 'I'm glad to hear it. I was worried that you hadn't found the drawer with the emergency supplies.'

She closed the door against the elements and crossed her arms, aware of how her teddy-bear nightshirt ended several inches above her knees. 'I did. For your information, I also bought several new batteries at the store tonight. Other than the power outage, which has affected everyone in the neighborhood, things here are in tip-top condition.'

There was a sudden brilliant flash, setting into motion an instant chain reaction. A split second later a loud noise echoed through the house, followed by an explosion of glass.

CHAPTER SIX

BEN moved faster than Kelly had ever dreamed possible. He caught her up in his arms and practically dove into the safety of the kitchen, shielding her from the unknown threat with his body.

For a long moment she stood plastered against his frame. His face hovered near hers, his breath whispering across the bridge of her nose.

His mouth loomed dangerously close. Underneath the overwhelming scent of rain, surrounding her, a spicy masculine fragrance filled her lungs. A hint of butter-scotch lingered on his breath and her impulsive side begged for a taste.

She stirred herself to traverse the few millimeters, but something warm and wet on her leg diverted her attention.

Percy.

Kelly tensed, feeling both foolish and angry at herself. How could she think of kissing a man who held both her and her daughter in such little regard?

The water on his slicker slowly seeped through her nightshirt, cooling her body's ardor as effectively as a hard blast of chilly rain.

She hid behind a lofty tone. 'You can put me down now.'

He lowered her to the floor. His cautious movements suggested reluctance, but she disregarded the idea as ridiculous. Once she'd planted her stocking-clad feet on the linoleum floor she moved to the doorway between the two rooms and gasped in horror.

A large tree branch jutted into the living room through what used to be the plate-glass picture window.

Ben spoke over her shoulder. 'I'd say things aren't quite in the tip-top condition you described.'

She started forward, too stunned to speak. His hand on her shoulder brought her to an abrupt stop.

'You're not going in there without shoes. You'll cut yourself.'

'Oh. You're right.' Still dazed, her feet remained rooted to the floor. A gust of wind blew rain inside, turning the cozy room cold and damp. Goosebumps rose on her skin and she shivered.

Ben nudged her. 'Get dressed in something warm while I see what I can do.' He motioned to the broken window.

Without a word of protest she grabbed a candle, before hurrying to the bedroom. As she tugged on a pair of jeans and a shirt she tried to summon the fury she'd felt toward him earlier.

It was impossible, thanks to the most recent and more pressing problem.

Her mind raced with the tasks to be done. The tree limb had to be removed and the window boarded shut. She hadn't taken a good enough look to see if a fallen branch had caused the damage or if the entire tree had toppled over.

She hoped it was the former.

Although she could deal with the situation herself, she found Ben's presence extremely reassuring. Only because he was the landlord, she told herself. She didn't need rescu*ing* any more than he apparently liked being cast in the role of rescu*er*.

Just as she was about to tiptoe from the room with her candle, a four-legged shadow rubbed against her thigh. Percy stopped near the edge of Carlie's bed and studied the sleeping child, before turning his gaze on Kelly. He cocked his head in silent query, as if asking permission.

'Go ahead,' she whispered, motioning for the Dalmatian to join her daughter. 'Just this once.' Although she didn't appreciate having pet hair on her hand-made quilt, at least Carlie would appreciate his comforting presence.

Percy scrambled onto the bed. Although he was a large animal he didn't disturb Carlie as he lay close to her huddled form. He placed his head on his paws as if determined to snatch a few winks of sleep before his master called him.

His master.

Kelly wondered if Ben would be upset by Percy's obvious devotion to Carlie. Perhaps he'd prefer his four-footed companion to be at his side, rather than lying next to a little girl.

Tough, she decided as she closed the bedroom door behind her. Ben would just have to grin and bear her company instead.

She strode into the living room and placed her candle on a table away from the draft. The chill had grown in the past five minutes and goosebumps once again rose on her flesh. She located a jacket in the closet near the entrance and slid into its warmth. The wind whistled as it swirled past the jagged pieces of glass still affixed to the window-frame.

Other than the sound of rain, spattering against the roof, the house was quiet. Too quiet.

She poked her head into the kitchen. It was empty. For the time being Ben was gone.

She grabbed a plastic trash can and found a pair of work gloves, before advancing towards the broken window. Glass crunched under her trainers and she winced at the thought of the damage she might have inflicted upon her stockinged feet if Ben hadn't stopped her.

She trained her light on the sofa and gasped. The heavy limb was resting on its back, the weight crumpling the frame as if the couch had been made of matchsticks. Twigs had sliced the upholstery into ribbons.

Glass glittered like diamonds on the floor. She picked up a number of pieces and dropped them into the trash can, leaving the tiny ones for the vacuum. No doubt she'd find shards in the shaggy carpeting and furniture for weeks to come. It wouldn't be safe for Carlie to play on the floor.

The next few steps brought her to the branch. Water droplets on the leaves shimmered under the low-intensity beam and dripped onto the carpeting.

It was an eerie sight.

The more she studied the destruction the more grateful she was for providentially sending Carlie to bed early. The branch could have killed them if they'd started another game.

The enormity of the situation suddenly soaked into her brain. Her body shook at the thought of their near miss and she sank onto the opposite recliner, her knees rubbing against a leafy twig. The flashlight trembled as her hands developed an uncontrollable palsy. A wide range of emotions surged through her—everything from fear and horror to thankfulness.

Sorting through her tangled morass of feelings, she placed the torch on her lap and rested her head in her hands as a few tears trickled down her cheeks. Her life in Sundance seemed to be spinning out of control. She'd never been plagued with such devastating misfortunes before.

The door slammed, heralding a visitor. She raised her head as Ben strode toward her, dropping his equipment near her feet. The dim lighting was enough to reveal tension on his face. 'What's wrong? Are you hurt?'

Kelly brushed away the moisture with the back of her hand as she shook her head. 'I'm fine.'

His tone possessed a definite edge. 'Is it Carlie?'

'She's fine. Percy's sleeping with her.'

He crouched beside her, his brow furrowed. 'Then...'

She forced a smile. 'It's nothing. I just realized what a close call we had. We'd been playing cards.' Her voice shook and she cleared her throat.

'Carlie had been sitting on the sofa. If I hadn't sent her to bed, or if this had happened twenty minutes earlier...' The rest of her sentence died, unspoken.

Ben grabbed her hand and tucked it in his. Although she still wore the work gloves, she wasn't immune to his touch. 'But it didn't so don't think about it.'

'I'm trying, but—'

'That's an order.' His smile belied the command. 'What ifs don't count.'

'You're right. They don't.' Kelly inhaled a shaky breath as she rose. 'What should we work on first?'

Straightening, Ben eyed her small frame. 'I doubt if you can—'

She widened her stance. 'I can do whatever is necessary.'

He opened his mouth, then closed it as if he'd decided not to belabor the point. 'I can't move the tree limb. It's too heavy. I'm going to saw off enough branches so we can tack a tarpaulin over the window. The canvas should keep out most of the rain for tonight.'

'You're going to use a chain saw during an electrical storm?' she asked, revealing how ridiculous she considered the idea.

His mouth twisted into a wry grin. 'The lightning's

stopped and it isn't raining very hard right now. The roof's overhang should give me enough protection.'

He retrieved the saw from where he'd placed it, then went outside. A minute later the distinct buzz of its motor filled the air as he set to work.

Kelly resumed her chore of picking up the large sections of glass. The branch in the window-frame wiggled.

'Stand back,' he commanded through the opening.

Unable to help, she retreated a few steps while he pulled on his end of the limb.

More glass gave way and something bit her cheek.

'Stand back,' Ben repeated. 'I've almost got it.'

She moved again. Leaves rustled and rain droplets flew in all directions as he pulled the branch completely outside. A gaping hole, leafy twigs and chunks of glass were left in its wake.

She yanked the hood of her jacket over her head, grabbed the metal toolbox he'd brought and went outside.

Rain fell at a steady pace, but without the pounding force exhibited an hour earlier. She stood behind Ben and waited for instructions.

He turned. 'What are you doing out here?'

'Helping you.'

'Go inside. You'll get all wet.'

'And you won't?'

'I'm wearing—'

'Look. We can stand out here and argue or get the job done,' she said impatiently. 'You can't tack the tarp to the window and hold your supplies at the same time. Besides, someone needs to point the light so you don't tack your thumb to the wall. Or can you see in the dark?' She raised one eyebrow, daring him to argue.

'Unless you've trained Percy to act as your assistant, you're stuck with me,' she added.

'OK. Let's get on with this.'

'My thoughts exactly,' she muttered under her breath.

Thanks to his size, he was able to tack the blue tarpaulin to the top of the window, without using a ladder. Kelly held the light with one hand and the nails in the other. Halfway through their job her teeth began to chatter, but she clamped her jaw shut.

She refused to be sent indoors; she would do her share.

At long last Ben had stretched the canvas over the opening. 'It's nothing fancy, but at least it will stop the wind and the rain from doing more damage inside.'

He took one look at her, then tugged the flashlight out of her unresisting grasp to shine it on her face. 'You're bleeding.'

She pulled off a glove to touch her cheek. Her fingers felt a scab. 'Not any more. A sliver of glass must have hit me.'

'You're frozen too.'

'Chilled.' She corrected him through stiff lips. 'A cup of hot coffee and I'll be fine.'

He swore something she couldn't make out and didn't want to. 'Go inside. I'll put my things in the truck.'

She wanted to tell him that everything was under control and he didn't have to stay. Her mouth, however, refused to work.

Inside the house she shrugged off her rain-soaked jacket and draped it over a kitchen chair, before removing her equally wet trainers.

Rubbing her arms, she glanced around the kitchen. Too bad every appliance needed electricity. Something hot to drink—soup, coffee, tea, *anything*—sounded like heaven. Unfortunately, it was anybody's guess as to when the power would be restored. It could be within minutes or hours. She hoped it wouldn't be days.

She carried every candle she owned from the living room into the kitchen. The glow of six small flames generated enough light to send the darkness retreating to the far corners of the room.

The front door opened, then closed with a quiet click. A heavy tread heralded Ben's presence before he strode into the candlelit kitchen as if he owned the place.

Which he did, she thought wryly.

He plunked a tall Thermos on the counter. 'Where are your coffee-cups?'

His take-charge attitude didn't escape her notice, but she couldn't refuse his request. 'Is that what I think it is?' she asked, opening a cupboard and removing two mugs.

'It is if you're thinking coffee.' Ben stripped off his slicker and draped it over another chair.

'I am. How did you manage to make something hot?'

'When I went home for my tools my electricity had come on again. I took time to make a pot in case the crews hadn't restored the power at this end of town.'

His consideration seemed out of character after he'd brushed them off as insignificant at the store a few hours earlier. 'Thanks for thinking of it.'

She passed a steaming mug to him. His supple fingers closed over hers and she wanted to purr like a kitten from the pleasure of the warmth enveloping her cold hands. In fact, his whole body emanated a heat that spanned the arm's length between them.

Unbidden, she responded like a four-o'clock flower as it opened its petals to the summer sun's afternoon rays. Her skin became extremely sensitive, reminding her of her missing camisole.

The thought of those warm, agile fingers, removing the lightweight fabric and caressing her body, sent her temperature rocketing. Shaken by her mental vision, her hands shook and she sloshed the coffee out of his mug.

'Still cold?'

'Yes,' she lied, releasing his cup to pick up her own. To admit what really ailed her would be the height of stupidity. It was totally illogical for him to stir her soul in a way she'd always wanted to experience. After all, she and Ben mixed like oil and water.

He moved to the deacon's bench. Sitting down, he patted the spot beside him. 'Come here.'

She hesitated, instinctively knowing what he intended. He'd bring her in close, tuck her against his chest and rub life back into her arms. Unfortunately, his touch affected her far too much to allow her to endure it under platonic circumstances. She wanted something more. Something that satisfied her feminine needs, every last one of them.

'I won't bite,' he said.

Kelly gave a half-hearted smile. Think of him as Tom's brother, not the most intriguing, virile male you've ever met.

'Come here.' He spoke softly.

His words seemed more invitation than order, but she couldn't stop her feet from shuffling forward any more than she could stop the storm outside. His baritone drew her as if invisible cords pulled them together—cords too strong to break.

She didn't want to try.

Ben watched her approach like a wary doe, and wondered what thoughts were running through her mind. It wasn't wise to invite her to sit next to him, not when her lips were blue with cold and he wanted to kiss them until they turned rosy red.

It wasn't wise when he'd learned earlier that only a thin cotton shirt shielded her nakedness from view.

It wasn't wise when he ached with a need he'd suppressed these past few years. He'd resisted the temptation she'd presented before, but he wasn't made of forged steel.

It especially wasn't wise because his brother had designs on her for himself.

Yet Tom was gone and he wasn't. Also, her finger was bare.

He gave himself a mental shake. Regardless of the lack of a ring, he knew Tom's intentions. There wasn't a woman alive who was worth the destruction of a close brotherly relationship. He'd treat Kelly Evers like he'd treat a patient—with objectivity.

However, as she sat beside him his plans dissolved as fast as instant coffee granules. Under the fresh, clean scent of rain her hair smelled of a summer garden and her reddish-gold tresses flowed across his chest like molten honey.

Ben pulled her close, wanting to share his warmth. She trembled. He set the mug on his other side, then surrounded her with his arms, stroking her chilled skin as if petting a frightened kitten.

Kelly rested her head against his shoulder and for the next few minutes he reveled in the feel of her body against his. Parts of him throbbed with a shockingly intense desire. Heat pooled below his belt until he thought himself capable of starting a brush fire with a simple touch.

He shifted positions, trying to ease the ache in his groin. At the same time he focused his thoughts on something other than the petite woman in his embrace.

Before he could settle her against him again she withdrew. In the next instant she'd skittered across the kitchen to stand near the counter, clutching her mug in a white-knuckled grip.

'Everything's in order,' she said brightly. Too brightly, he thought. 'I'm sure you're in a hurry to leave so I'll get Percy.'

She moved past him, but he cut her off before she reached the door.

'You're coming with me.'

Kelly stared at him, her eyes puzzled, her brow furrowed. Then her expression cleared.

'No.'

'No?'

She shook her head. 'That's what I said.'

'You can't stay here.'

'And why not?'

He raised one eyebrow. 'Your power is out which means you don't have heat.'

'This is June, not December. We can dress warmly. By morning everything will be back to normal.'

'You hope,' he finished. 'It depends on how badly the storm affected the rest of the town.'

'Then we'll wait our turn.'

Seeing the now-familiar stubborn set to her jaw, his frustration level rose. 'Why are you being so difficult about this?'

'Because we've already been an inconvenience to you. You fixed the window—you don't have any other obligation toward us.' She drew a deep breath. 'In any case, we've had this argument before.'

'Yes, and I won,' he said smugly, still standing within inches of her. 'If you're worried about your reputation, don't be. I'll explain about you and Tom being engaged.'

'Engaged?' Her face registered supreme shock.

'Yes. No one will give it a second thought,' he reassured her.

'Where did you get the idea that Tom and I—?'

'Are an item?' he finished for her. 'From Tom.'

She blinked, then shook her head in apparent disbelief. 'Tom said that? When?'

Ben's thoughts whirled as he tried to recall his brother's exact words. 'Before you'd moved to town he dropped by for a visit. At the time he explained how he was hoping you'd become part of the family. I assumed—'

'Wrong,' she said flatly. 'Tom and I are friends.'

'Friends?' he asked, aware of how loosely the term could be applied to a variety of relationships.

She nodded. '*Only* friends. Why, he hasn't even...' Her voice died. Her skin turned a rosy hue as she backed up two steps and stared at the floor.

Although Ben suspected what she'd started to say, curiosity propelled him to ask, 'He hasn't even what?'

She hardly spoke above a whisper. 'Kissed me.'

For some reason Ben found extreme satisfaction in her confession. He crossed the distance between them in one long stride and placed his arms around her. Driven by need, he bent his head and planted his lips against hers.

She stiffened, then relaxed to lean into him. Her mouth opened and he groaned at the sweetness he found within.

He pressed her closer, filling the hollows of her body with his like two interlocking pieces of a puzzle. He hadn't wanted anyone to such a degree since Alyce had left him.

Alyce. Her name was as chilling as a bucket of ice water dumped on his head. He pulled back. Would he ever be free of the impact she'd made on his life?

For a long moment they stared at each other. The shadows on her face seemed more pronounced than they had a few minutes ago, indicating an emotional retreat. Although she tried to break free of his hold he tightened it as he mulled over the situation.

He narrowed his eyes as he studied her. 'Why would Tom tell me that he wanted you to be part of the family if he wasn't interested in you?'

'It's obvious,' she snapped. 'He's matchmaking.'

Once again Ben recalled snippets of the conversation with his brother. He remembered accusing Tom of chasing after older women and Tom hadn't denied it. Apparently, though, Tom knew him far better than Ben thought he did. Ben would have refused a blind date without a qualm.

Asking him to look after his potential sister-in-law, however, was a different story. Without any pressure of a deep relationship, a mutual attraction would blossom between Kelly and himself—or so Tom clearly hoped.

To think that he'd believed Tom incapable of strategic planning. His younger brother had played him like a well-used violin. Ben couldn't decide if he should be angry or commend Tom for his tactics.

'He and his girlfriend were always setting me up with his friends,' Kelly said. 'Trying to, I should say. I went out a few times, but Carlie never seemed to hit it off with any of the guys. So we never went past the first date.' She shrugged.

'I see.'

The usual sparkle in her eyes disappeared, leaving them dull and lifeless. 'Tom asked you to check on us, didn't he?'

He nodded slowly.

Her sigh was long and deep. 'Things are definitely making sense now.' She squared her shoulders. 'I hereby release you from any responsibility or obligation toward us. Please go before Carlie wakes up and sees you.'

'Why don't you want Carlie to know I'm here?'

Kelly's composure visibly cracked under his gaze.

Clearly the stress of the day had taken its toll. 'Because I won't allow you to hurt her any more.'

He was stunned by her accusation. 'What have I done?'

She tossed her head and scoffed. 'Don't insult my intelligence. Your inconsideration is obvious to a blind person.'

'Wait a minute—' he began, but she interrupted.

'Carlie is a little girl who craves the male companionship missing in her life. For some reason she's formed some sort of bond with you and believes you're the best thing since ice cream. And yet, time after time, you've rejected her.' Kelly crossed her arms. 'If you need me to paint you a picture I have plenty of examples.'

Kelly was right. He'd done his best to distance himself from the child's affections.

'She doesn't understand why you blow hot then cold and, quite frankly, neither do I. Therefore it's best if our paths don't cross. I can't—*won't*—make excuses for your behavior any more.'

He spoke softly. 'What has Tom told you about me?'

She tapped her stockinged foot. 'Obviously not enough.'

'I'm serious,' he insisted. 'What has he told you?'

Kelly shrugged as if the facts she'd been given weren't noteworthy. 'Just that you're divorced. A workaholic. A brilliant diagnostician.'

'Then he hasn't said anything about...' He hesitated.

'About what?'

He looked directly into her eyes. 'About my daughter?'

CHAPTER SEVEN

'YOUR...daughter?' Kelly choked out the words. Why hadn't she heard this before?

Ben nodded, his eyes pain-filled.

Amazed, she sank onto the bench. 'Tom never mentioned you had—have—a child. Where is she?'

He sat beside her. 'I'll start at the beginning. After my residency I became devoted to my new practice. My patients called me at all hours of the day or night and I never turned anyone down. Alyce—my wife—couldn't understand why I spent so much time at the office and hospital.'

He threaded his fingers together in a tight fist. 'I felt such pride over reaching my goal—my dream of practicing medicine was finally reality. People needed me and, sadly enough, my ego wouldn't let me turn anyone away. I cared for my patients at the expense of my family.'

Ben paused and Kelly waited for him to continue. A nearby candle flickered, creating a perfect ghostly backdrop for the revealing of secrets.

'Tanya was nine at the time everything came to a head. According to Alyce, she'd complained of a stomach-ache for weeks. I did the usual tests and didn't find anything conclusive. I was certain it was nothing. Alyce had a tendency to overdramatize situations, especially illnesses. She considered everything a major disaster when most people would consider those same incidents as minor inconveniences. Eventually, I began dismissing her complaints.'

'But this time something *was* wrong,' Kelly guessed.

He nodded. 'I'd been called to the hospital for a patient with pneumonia. Alyce had left a message that Tanya was vomiting. It was during flu season, and from the symptoms Alyce gave me I assumed Tanya had caught the same bug as everyone else. After giving her the usual spiel, I stayed at the hospital until my patient was out of danger. Unfortunately, by the time I came home Tanya's fever was astronomical.'

'Appendix?'

'Yes. By the time she'd arrived in Spearfish her appendix had ruptured. Peritonitis set in. The next few days were the worst of my life. Naturally, Alyce blamed me, and rightly so. I should have been more alert.'

'You don't know that. Not all appendicitis cases are straightforward.'

'No, but if I'd let my partner take care of the pneumonia patient I'd have been home and could have diagnosed her sooner.'

'Were you on call?'

'Yes.'

Kelly shrugged. 'Then it was the luck of the draw. Tanya could have easily been ill on a night when you weren't on duty.'

'The point is she wasn't.'

Certain she wouldn't change his mind, she steered the conversation forward. 'What happened next?'

His shoulders heaved with his deep breath. 'Tanya recovered. On the day the surgeon released her from the hospital Alyce served me with divorce papers. She said I already had a wife and family—medicine and my patients—and couldn't handle another set. She was right.'

'Where are they now?' Kelly asked, somewhat relieved by Tanya's happy ending.

'Alyce and her husband—he's an accountant—live in Denver.'

Kelly wasn't surprised to hear that Alyce's second husband had a nine-to-five job. 'And Tanya? Do you see her?'

'Not very often. I call every few weeks, visit her whenever I can get away.'

'Does she ever come to Wyoming?'

'Two summers ago she was here for a month. She's thirteen now and would rather spend time with her friends. She has a life--I don't want to interfere.'

The idea that he'd given up his daughter so easily didn't sit well with Kelly. It reminded her too much of Slade. 'Maybe you should,' she said tartly. 'Regardless of how great that life appears, she doesn't have her father.'

He looked taken aback at her sharp tone, but she didn't care. 'Now you know the sordid details. I don't mean to reject Carlie,' he said slowly. 'I think she's a great kid, but...'

'She reminds you of Tanya? Or are you just afraid to get close to a child?'

He cleared his throat. 'A little of both, I think. In any case, I don't intend to have a family again.'

His affirmation pained her. 'Don't you want one?'

'It isn't a matter of what I want. It's a case of juggling my personal responsibilities with my professional ones. I've already proved that I can't.'

'That's ridiculous!'

'You sound like Tom. He's been after me for the past two years to resume what he calls a normal life, but I won't. At least not until I find someone who is extremely independent and can make decisions without me.'

Kelly felt as if he'd slapped her in the face. From the very first time she'd met him he'd had to rescue her from one situation after another. Obviously he didn't classify her as independent or capable of making decisions on her own.

'Well, I hope you enjoy your lonely life.' She walked around the kitchen, blowing out all but two of the candles. 'It's late. You'd better go.'

'You're angry.'

'Disappointed,' she corrected. 'You've allowed yourself to carry the guilt Alyce dumped on you and you'll continue to do so. The only problem is that everyone pays the price, everyone except Alyce.

'Tanya is missing out on a wonderful relationship with her father and you're too busy blaming yourself to have a personal relationship with anyone else. Maybe you made a mistake and maybe you didn't, but letting it rule the rest of your life won't change a thing, except make you a bitter old man.'

'Those are strong words.'

'Yes, they are,' she said, refusing to back down.

He leaned back and folded his arms across his chest. 'Well, Ms Psychology, what makes you an expert?'

'You're like Carlie's father. Too cowardly to face responsibilities, you totally ignore them.'

He squared his jaw. 'I beg your pardon.'

'It's true,' she insisted. 'You should be fighting to establish a relationship with your daughter. I'll bet you didn't even argue over custody.'

The pulse throbbed at his temple—she'd struck home. Suddenly she felt compelled to spill her own secrets.

'Slade walked out of Carlie's life without a whimper. In fact, he left months before she was born. He didn't even have the courage to give her his legal name.' Her voice cracked and she swallowed the frog in her throat.

Silence descended and the darkness seemed to close

in around her. Her energy now spent, her shoulders slumped. 'I'll get Percy so you can leave.'

He shot to his feet. 'I won't go without you.'

She counted to ten. 'Look, we've already travelled this path. Let it drop. Carlie and I can take care of ourselves. We aren't your responsibility.'

'What would you have done if I hadn't come by tonight?'

'I don't know,' she admitted, 'but I would have thought of something.'

He ran both hands through his hair. 'Woman, you're absolutely—'

'Mommy?' a small voice said from the doorway. Carlie stood there with Percy beside her as she rubbed her eyes.

Kelly approached her daughter. 'Yes, sweetie?'

'I had an accident.'

Suddenly the overhead lights came on. Kelly blinked owlishly as her pupils adjusted to the brightness.

'Change your clothes,' she told Carlie once her eyes recovered. 'I'll take care of your bed in a minute.'

The child disappeared around the corner and Kelly turned to Ben. 'They've restored the power so you can leave with a clear conscience. Goodnight.'

Without waiting for his reply, she hurried into Carlie's room and stripped the calico quilt off her bed. To her surprise, Ben followed. Without a word he untucked the sheets and wadded them into a ball.

'I can do this *myself*,' she ground out. 'I've changed linen on my own for years.'

'Then you can enjoy the novelty of having someone help,' he said, tossing the lightweight quilt over a chair. 'Where is the extra bedding?'

Kelly stooped to retrieve floral-printed sheets and a clean pad from the dresser's bottom drawer. Ben went to the other side and helped her tug the thick pad over the corners.

'Carlie must not have accidents very often,' he said.

'No, she doesn't. Why do you ask?'

He pulled the fitted sheet into place. 'Most mothers resort to using waterproof liners. You haven't.'

Kelly unfolded the top sheet and Ben helped her smooth it across the mattress. 'She just started having a problem the past few weeks. I'd meant to wake her for a trip to the bathroom but, with everything happening like it did, I forgot.'

'Maybe she has an infection,' he suggested.

Her hands stilled. 'I never thought of that.' She hoped it was something so easily treated.

'Run a urinalysis in the morning and a culture if it's indicated.'

'I will.'

'Do you have a doctor?'

'Not in Sundance.'

'Then send me a copy of the results. If she needs an antibiotic I'll be glad to prescribe one.'

'Thanks.'

Carlie appeared in the doorway with the Dalmatian beside her. 'Can I stay up now and play with Percy? I'm not tired.' She struggled to stifle a yawn.

'Percy's going home now,' Kelly said, throwing Ben a pointed glance.

Carlie climbed into bed. 'Will you bring him back again, Dr Ben?'

He smiled. 'Yes, I will.' Holding up his hands to forestall her next question, he added, 'We'll try for Saturday.'

A horrendous clap of thunder resounded. Once again the house was plunged into darkness.

'Mommy?' Carlie wailed.

'Stay in bed,' Kelly ordered. 'I'm going to look for a flashlight. She stretched out her arm to grope her way to the door and stumbled over Percy.

Immediately Ben caught her. For a long minute she remained plastered to his massive chest until her feet found solid ground.

Even then she couldn't force herself to move. Being in his arms on a dark and stormy night was more comforting and far more appealing than she cared to admit.

'Mommy!' Carlie wailed again.

The cellular phone hooked to Ben's belt warbled. While he answered, Kelly fled in the direction she'd last seen the torch.

She returned to find Percy curled on the bed next to Carlie and Ben replacing the phone on his belt.

'Thanks to the lightning, there's been a rock slide across the road at Devil's Tower,' he reported. 'It caused a collision between several cars. Ambulances were dispatched and should arrive here in about thirty minutes.'

'How bad are the injured?'

'I haven't heard. But the hospital switchboard can't get through to Dee. Someone has to cover the lab in case we need blood crossmatched.'

'I'd go, but—' She motioned toward Carlie.

'Bring her along,' he said. 'We'll find a spare bed somewhere. If nothing else, there's a cot in the doctors' lounge.'

Kelly came to an instant decision. 'Percy can stay with her in my department. That way she won't be alone.'

'Fair enough. I'll start the truck and get the heater going.' He left the room before she could offer to take her own vehicle.

'Come on, Carlie. Let's put on some warm clothes. You're coming with us.'

'Percy too?'

'Percy too. Now hurry.'

She dressed Carlie in record time and rushed through the house to the front door, where Ben was waiting. Without a word Ben dropped his slicker over Carlie's head, before swinging her into his arms. Kelly and Percy followed them out to Ben's four-wheel-drive pick-up.

'I'll take my own van,' she said.

Ben continued to walk as if he hadn't heard her, then opened the door to his truck and allowed Carlie to slide inside.

Frustrated by his dictatorial methods, she entered on the passenger side. 'I'd prefer driving myself,' she began.

He started the engine. 'Do you have a four-wheel drive?'

'No, but—'

'Then don't argue.'

Giving the broken tree in her yard only a passing glance, Kelly focused her attention on the road ahead. Tree limbs of varying sizes littered the streets and water ran along the curbs like a raging river.

'Looks like everyone's going to be cleaning their yards this weekend,' Ben remarked, as he dodged another downed branch.

'Including us.'

Ben slowed to avoid more fallen branches, but water flooded the intersection directly ahead. He braked to a stop. 'We'll have to backtrack.'

Peering over his shoulder, he reversed the vehicle and turned right to drive down another street.

They didn't get far, before encountering another obstacle. He swore under his breath.

'We may have to walk,' Kelly said. 'How far away from the hospital are we?'

'A quarter of a mile or so. I just hope the ambulance

can get through.' He opened his phone with one hand while he steered with the other. 'Dial the ER number for me, will you?'

Kelly reached across Percy and Carlie for the unit. The heater was warming the truck's cab and she caught a distinct odor of Percy's wet hair mingling with Carlie's strawberry bath scent. Quite a combination.

After she'd punched the numbers she handed the phone back to Ben.

'We're on our way, but several streets are blocked by either tree limbs or water,' he told the person at the other end of the line. 'It'll take us a while to get there. By the way, Kelly's with me so don't bother trying to contact Dee.'

He listened intently, then said goodbye. 'According to Cheryl, the city crews have cleared part of the emergency route. If I can get onto it we'll be home free.'

Kelly didn't say a word. No comment was required. Instead, she clutched Carlie closer to her side.

Ben's headlights revealed another huge branch stretched across the pavement several yards ahead. His face appeared etched in stone as he slowed to a crawl and surveyed his options.

Kelly ventured a guess. 'We can't get past it, can we?'

He downshifted. 'We will. Hang on.'

Bracing her feet on the floorboard, Kelly hung onto Carlie. The truck tipped to the left and then the right as Ben eased the front wheels over the curb and onto someone's lawn. Before long he eased the vehicle down the curb until all four tires made contact with the pavement.

'Can we do that again?' Carlie asked, obviously thrilled by the experience of bouncing from side to side.

'I hope not,' Kelly said fervently.

Ben grinned at her over Carlie's head before he re-addressed his attention to the road. 'No sense of adventure, I see. Does this mean you don't want to go off-roading with me?'

'Thanks, but, no, thanks.'

'Still wish you'd driven yourself?'

'At the risk of feeding your ego, I'm glad I didn't,' she said honestly. 'We wouldn't have made it on our own.'

'Glad to be of service.'

The hospital loomed directly ahead. Strategically placed lights shone like beacons. The surrounding houses were conspicuously dark.

'Our emergency generator supplies power to the critical areas,' Ben said as he pulled into the doctors' parking lot behind the ER entrance. 'Most, if not all, of the lab is hooked to it too.'

Kelly nodded in understanding.

The driveway leading to the ER was clear—not a vehicle or person stood in sight. 'Good,' Ben said, sounding satisfied. 'We beat the ambulances.'

'I'm glad too.' She wanted to see Carlie settled and have time to check out her equipment. If the electrical storm had rendered her instruments inoperable, she needed to know before a deluge of patients, requiring her services, flooded the hospital.

Kelly hopped out of the truck, shivering under the unwelcome onslaught of cold wind and rain. She turned to reach for Carlie, but Ben took her daughter in his arms and strode toward the canopy's protection.

Kelly followed, with Percy trotting beside her. Inside the hallway Ben set Carlie on her feet.

'I'll be right back,' Kelly said. 'I hope no one complains because Carlie and Percy came along.'

'If anyone does *I'll* deal with them,' he stated firmly.

Kelly grabbed Carlie's hand and hurried around the corner to her section. After showing Carlie to the parti-

tioned area containing the bed and removing the bor-
rowed slicker, Kelly located an extra sheet to use as a
blanket.

'Percy will stay with you so don't be afraid. I'll be in
the other room or around the corner. OK?'

Carlie nodded. 'Can he sleep with me?'

Changing another set of sheets was a small price to
pay for Carlie's—and Percy's—co-operation. While no
one might comment on a dog in the hospital, it would
be totally different if the animal ran loose through the
hallways.

'I suppose. Now, I'll close this door so the light won't
bother you. Remember, I'll be nearby so don't be
scared.'

'I won't,' the child declared. 'Percy will p'tect me.'

Kelly bent to kiss her on the cheek. 'Good girl. I'll
wake you when it's time to leave.'

'G'night, Mommy.'

Kelly slipped into the testing area just as the wail of
an ambulance siren died. She flicked a few switches to
bring her equipment out of standby mode. Knowing the
ER staff needed time to assess their patients, she ran a
series of checks on each system to verify its accuracy.
Satisfied with her findings, she headed for the ER.

Adrenaline rushed through her as she anticipated the
unknown. The night was just beginning.

Ben slipped his arms through the protective gear as he
spoke. 'How many casualties?'

Cheryl tied the strings of his gown. 'Three. All tour-
ists. According to the initial report from the scene, the
oldest man has thoracic and abdominal trauma. His wife
has broken bones and the other fellow has bumps and
bruises.'

'Notify Spearfish to stand by for possible surgery.'

'I already did.' She nudged him good-naturedly with her elbow. 'Nice-looking group you brought along.'

He grinned. Cheryl was an old friend so he didn't take offense at her comment. 'I was at her place anyway.'

Cheryl raised one eyebrow. 'You don't say.'

'Kelly moved into my rental house. With the power out, I stopped by to check on them.'

'And how were they?'

'Fine. At least until a tree branch broke through a window.'

Cheryl's smile was broad. 'Ben Shepard to the rescue. You'd better be careful. People will think you're starting to give up your hermit's life.'

He froze. 'A hermit?'

She shrugged. 'What else would you call it? No one sees you anywhere but here at the hospital or at your office. You haven't attended any social engagements in recent years, not even the staff Christmas parties.'

'I get out,' he protested. 'I jog, I go to church and the grocery store. I've even gone to the movie theater.'

She dismissed his objection with a wave of her hand. 'Those places don't count because you go alone. As far as the eligible women are concerned, you live like a monk.'

If she only knew... His thoughts towards Kelly Evers didn't fall in the 'monk' category, although he wished they would. He wasn't ready to risk the potential pain associated with failure.

Her face turned serious. 'I don't know Kelly at all, but if she's the one to bring you back from the purgatory you've put yourself in these past few years then she's got to be one great gal.'

She continued in a lighter vein. 'Besides, you're going to need a woman who'll let you keep around that miniature horse you call a dog. How you can stand to have an animal in the house, shedding hair all over the furniture, is beyond my understanding.'

'Hey, pets are therapeutic.' He pretended affront.

'So is gardening.' She cocked her head as the familiar siren grew louder then died abruptly. 'They're here.'

Replacing their friendly banter with solemnity, Cheryl and Ben rushed to the ambulance entrance. Two other nurses joined them.

'This guy is the worst of the three,' the EMT reported, as he flung open the double doors at the back of his vehicle. 'His car hit the rock pile and flipped over three times. He was complaining of chest and abdominal pain. Also difficulty in breathing.'

The technician monitoring the patient jumped out, holding the IV bag of saline. The group pulled the stretcher forward until the folded wheels locked into their rolling position.

Immediately Ben noticed the cervical collar and the airway. The second EMT began reciting the vital sign readings before he ended with, 'He's wearing a medical alert bracelet for diabetes.'

'Somebody, check it out,' Ben ordered. A nurse rushed to obey. 'Let's get him inside. Where are the others?'

'A few minutes behind us.'

In no time at all the group entered the trauma room and Ben assessed his patient, watching the man's non-verbal responses for cues. The labored breathing, the decreased sounds from the right lung and complaints of chest pain suggested a pneumothorax. The bruises, abdominal distension and rigidity pointed to internal trauma. His patient needed a trip to the closest surgery suite as soon as possible.

Over the next several minutes Ben worked to relieve the man's labored breathing. As soon as he'd inserted a chest tube to equalize the pressure he saw a marked clinical improvement.

'Start another IV,' Ben ordered. 'And I want someone watching his airway at all times.' He glanced around the room. 'Where's X-Ray?'

'Vern's on his way,' Cheryl said, opening another intravenous kit.

Kelly slipped across the threshold and he beckoned her forward. 'I want blood gases,' he told her, 'a CBC, chemistry panel, and a crossmatch for four units of blood. We'll catheterize him for a urinalysis.'

She nodded and began to draw the necessary blood samples before Cheryl inserted the second fluid line.

'Hand me a syringe. I'll do the arterial puncture,' he said. Expecting an argument, he was surprised when Kelly gave him none. By the time she'd finished filling the tubes she needed he had the sample ready and waiting.

The sound of activity in the hallway drifted through the open doors. A graduate nurse bustled into their room—a young brunette who'd finished training and was waiting to hear if she'd passed her Board of Nursing exam. 'The second ambulance is here,' she said.

'Is Allen around?' he asked, referring to the physician's assistant who normally staffed the ER.

'The nursing home called him earlier, but he's here now.'

The radiology technician rushed in and Ben stated his request. 'I want chest and abdominal films, stat.'

His orders given, Ben entered the waiting portion of the game. He stepped away from the patient to allow Vern and the support staff enough space to work. In the meantime, he'd use these moments to jot down his notes.

'Do we have a name yet?' he asked no one in particular.

'Ted Cranston,' an ambulance attendant supplied. 'His wife says they're from Minnesota.'

Ten minutes ticked by. Anxious for a preliminary lab report, Ben strode toward the nurses' station and a telephone. On the way Allen White, a portly man who was Ben's contemporary, came out of a second exam room.

'How are things in there?' Ben asked.

'The wife has a broken ulna and radius, and possible rib fractures. I'm waiting for the X-rays. The other guy has a knot on his head and a headache that would stop a buffalo, but otherwise he's fine. I'm keeping him for observation, though.'

'Sounds good.'

'How's your fellow?'

'Punctured lung. Probable internal bleeding. I'll know how bad it is before long.'

Allen's face was grave. 'Want me to tell his wife?'

'I will as soon as I have a few more answers.'

Vern rushed forward, brandishing Radiology's oversized manila envelope. 'Here are the films.'

Ben stuffed the chest X-ray onto the view-box behind the nurses' station and flicked the light switch. One by one he reviewed the different views Vern had taken.

The films confirmed what he'd already suspected. One of several broken ribs had punctured the right lung and caused its partial collapse. The spleen was clearly damaged, bleeding into the abdominal cavity. He'd guessed as much, even without performing a peritoneal lavage.

He dialed the lab. 'Any results yet?' he asked.

'I have the blood gas and CBC finished,' Kelly said, reciting the numbers in her next breath. 'The chemistry tests will be done in a minute. Actually, they're printing right now. I can call you back if you like.'

'I'll wait.'

After a brief pause she began to relay more numbers, while Ben jotted them on the pad next to the phone.

He noted the abnormal figures for the liver enzymes and kidney tests, the low hematocrit and the red blood cells in the urine. The findings were definite—his patient had suffered extensive abdominal trauma and required immediate surgery.

'Thanks,' he told Kelly, before he hurried back to the trauma room.

'We'll send him to Rapid City instead of Spearfish,' he told the nurses. 'He needs a renal specialist, along with a surgeon. His kidneys look like they've been damaged too.'

'I'll call the helicopter.' Cheryl left to make the arrangements.

'Watch for shock,' he told the GN. 'As soon as the blood is crossmatched transfuse a unit.'

Ben strode toward the cubicle where Mrs Cranston was waiting. He found her lying on a stretcher and wearing a cervical collar, crying softly as she cradled her splinted left arm. Tears ravaged her sixtyish face, adding lines to the ones age had given her.

'Mrs Cranston?' he asked. 'I'm Dr Shepard.'

'My husband, Ted,' she choked out. 'How is he?'

He patted her shoulder. 'He's badly injured. His right lung is collapsed and he's bleeding internally. He'll need surgery.'

She gasped. 'Surgery?'

'They'll probably remove his spleen and repair any damage to his liver and kidneys. We're sending him to Rapid City via air ambulance. The specialists will take good care of him.'

'You know he has diabetes?'

'Yes. We're taking that into consideration. I'll keep you posted as soon as I know more.' He patted her good hand. 'We're doing everything we can for your husband so try to relax.'

Her smile was wan. 'I'd like to, but whenever I close my eyes I see those rocks, coming toward us.' She shivered.

'What happened?'

'We were trying to hurry back to our hotel. As we drove around Devil's Tower I saw something moving out of the corner of my eye. Rocks started bouncing across the road. Ted jerked the steering-wheel to avoid the oncoming car, but we hit it anyway. Then we slid off the road and started rolling. I shudder to think how bad it might have been if we hadn't been wearing our seat belts.'

Mrs Cranston shivered as if she were cold, then cleared her throat. 'I'm so glad the other driver had a cellphone to call for help. I've told my husband before that we need one when we travel, but he hasn't been convinced. I'm sure he is now, provided he lives through this.' She dabbed at her eyes with a tissue.

Ben's stomach knotted at a vision of Kelly and Carlie being in the same predicament without any means of communication. For his own peace of mind he wouldn't rest until she owned one. If need be, he'd purchase it himself.

It was nearly midnight by the time Ted Cranston left for the regional hospital at Rapid City. Cheryl had called in the social worker to locate the couple's family and arrange for his wife to join him.

The drama had ended. Ben strode to the lab in search of Kelly but only the quiet hum of the equipment greeted him.

He pushed open the door to the phlebotomy area and peeked around the partition. Kelly lay on her side, curled around Carlie, while Percy slept near their feet.

It was a picture of familial contentment—mother, daughter and dog—and it pained him not to be a part.

Was it possible to be given a second chance? Did he want to risk failure once again?

CHAPTER EIGHT

WHILE the city would feel the storm's influence for some time, life at the hospital went on as usual and Kelly focused her attention on the lab's budget woes.

'I'd like a copy of our shipping manifests and the corresponding invoices,' she told Vanessa Osbourne, the hospital's purchasing officer, on Friday morning.

Sitting behind her desk, Vanessa folded her manicured hands to show off the flashy diamonds affixed to nearly every finger on her hand. Wearing a tailored business suit and high heels, she was the epitome of a successful businesswoman.

Kelly felt frumpy in comparison, wearing a shapeless scrub suit and limp lab coat.

'Whatever for?' Vanessa asked, blinking as if amazed by the request. 'Are you able to interpret them?'

Wanting to wipe the smug look off the younger woman's face, Kelly faked her own smile. 'I think so. I'm sure I can read how many items a company shipped and how much they cost.'

'This is highly irregular,' Vanessa began.

Kelly was surprised by the woman's resistance. 'Is it? Seems like a good business practice. In fact, I think it should become current policy. After all, we're supposed to save money. The best way to accomplish our goal is for each manager to see what we're being charged.'

'Ed hasn't ever asked for this information.'

'Ed isn't part of the task force on fiscal responsibility,' Kelly reminded her.

Vanessa's red-lipsticked mouth formed a hard line and

she eyes glared at Kelly. 'Are you accusing me or the people in Accounting of not being able to add correctly?'

Dee had warned her of Vanessa's *tendre* for Hank Baxter, the head accountant.

'No,' Kelly said. 'I simply want to know what we're paying for our supplies. There may be other companies who can provide the same goods at a lower rate.'

Vanessa's shoulders squared. 'We've already negotiated your contract for the year. I've looked over the bids with Hank myself and we chose the cheapest supplier.' Her voice bristled. 'I suggest that you approach your problem from your end and not mine. In other words, Ms Evers, deal with your business and let us take care of ours.'

Kelly refused to back down. Whether this information would prove useful or not, she wanted to satisfy herself and the committee of her thoroughness. 'Then you refuse to give me copies of the invoices?'

'I assure you, everything is in order.'

Vanessa's evasion didn't escape Kelly's notice. 'I'm not implying that anyone has made a mistake. I'm only on a fact-finding mission.'

The woman's eyes narrowed as if she didn't believe Kelly's innocent statement.

Kelly rose, ready to play her trump card. 'The committee will meet again this afternoon. I hope I won't have to report on the lack of co-operation coming from your department.'

Vanessa's face appeared as hard as granite and her lips remained compressed into a thin line of disapproval. In spite of her skillfully applied make-up, her sour expression made her look older than her reported twenty-six years.

'I'll send those forms to you as soon as my staff gathers them,' Vanessa said stiffly.

Kelly stifled her desire to shout a resounding 'Yes!'. 'I think the records for the past six months should give me enough data to work with.'

'Suit yourself.' Vanessa picked up a gold-plated fountain pen and held it loosely in her fingers. 'By the way, how long will you be with us?'

Her sweet tone raised a warning flag. 'Until the end of August. About six weeks,' Kelly replied cautiously.

'Oh, my. That's not very long, is it?'

'No,' Kelly said, her stomach tensing at the direction of the conversation.

Vanessa inspected the red polish on her fingernails. 'Funny thing about contracts. They can be broken or simply not renewed. Especially if the person involved is difficult to work with, if you catch my drift.'

Kelly clenched her fists at her side. 'I do.'

'Good. I work closely with the human resources director too. I'm sure you'd hate for any unflattering comments to filter back to him, wouldn't you?' Her smile and voice were sickeningly sweet.

Kelly felt as if she'd been checkmated. She stared at the woman, refusing to cower under her thinly veiled threat.

'Then it's all the more important that I do a good job,' Kelly said, meeting the other woman's hateful gaze. 'I'll look forward to receiving those invoices.'

Without giving Vanessa another chance to speak, Kelly walked out of the room. Although her legs shook and her chest burned with emotion, she kept her pace slow and easy. It wouldn't do for the vengeful Vanessa Osbourne to see that she'd struck Kelly in her most vulnerable spot.

She held onto her composure until she reached the lab. Once there she sank onto a chair and covered her face with her hands.

'Vanessa's a bitch, isn't she?' Dee commiserated.

Kelly straightened. 'Why, Dee, I've never heard you talk like that.'

'I've lived too long not to call a spade a spade. That woman's poison. Pure, unadulterated poison.'

Her colleague's vehemence brought a smile to Kelly's face. 'She won't win any congeniality awards,' she agreed.

Dee plopped onto a chair beside her. 'Tell me what happened.'

Kelly gave her a brief rundown, finishing with Vanessa's threat.

'I wouldn't worry about your contract,' Dee said. 'She may try to throw her weight around, but too many people here think you're doing a marvelous job. She won't succeed.'

'I hope not.' It was bad enough to contemplate moving at the end of the summer—the prospect of not staying until then was unthinkable. 'But why was she so upset about showing me the invoices?'

Dee shrugged. 'She has an over-inflated view of herself—thinks she knows more than the rest of us.'

While Kelly found a note of truth in Dee's observation, Vanessa's actions puzzled her. 'Then I'd think she'd want to wave them under my nose to make me look ignorant.'

'Do you think something is wrong?'

'We've gone through our supply requirements with a fine-toothed comb,' Kelly reminded her. 'You said yourself that we don't have any fat to trim. We have to look at other options.'

'Do you think she'll co-operate?'

'I don't know.' She hoped Vanessa would—she didn't want to stage a repeat performance of today's meeting.

Still, she'd do whatever was necessary, no matter how distasteful or difficult it might be.

Dee paused. 'Dr Shepard's on the committee, isn't he?' At Kelly's nod she continued, 'Maybe you should discuss this with him, explain what you're trying to do. He'd get those invoices without any problem.'

Kelly knew he would. However, just once she'd like to show him that she could manage without his help. He'd already rescued her many times during her short tenure in Sundance. She didn't want to add another occasion to the list.

Besides, he prized independence in a woman as much as she did. Crying to him for help in overcoming Vanessa's opposition would simply reinforce his low opinion of her when she wanted to reverse it.

'For now I'll wait and see what develops.'

'Vanessa won't give in without a fight,' Dee predicted.

'Maybe. Maybe not. If she is hiding something and doesn't co-operate, people will wonder why.'

Dee slapped her thighs as she rose. 'Well, honey, good luck. But, if you ask me, since you're chummy with him anyway you should get Dr Shepard on your side. She won't dare cross him.'

'Chummy with him?' Kelly echoed. 'Who says?'

'Now, don't get your garters in a knot. You mentioned how he stopped by your place to check on you during last night's storm. Not many landlords would bother.'

Kelly's face warmed. 'I'm sure he looks after all of his tenants.'

Dee shook her head. 'Nope. My niece works for the Powder River Realty Company and manages his property. She handles everything from collecting the rent to organizing repairs. Few people ever meet Ben Shepard.'

'It's only because I'm a friend of his brother, Tom,'

Kelly insisted. 'Ben is only being kind. That's all.' She finished on a note which indicated that the subject was closed.

The idea Dee had planted in her mind was bitter-sweet. She'd like to believe her colleague's assertion that Ben was paying her special attention, but he had plainly outlined his matrimonial requirements.

From what she'd learned about Alyce, Kelly didn't resemble his ex-wife in appearance or temperament. What single parent *wasn't* independent? She had provided for Carlie for the past five years, dealing with every problem singlehandedly.

Unfortunately, Ben didn't see her self-sufficient side, and hadn't seen it from the very beginning. In his eyes she didn't meet his criteria, and to her deep regret she didn't know how to correct his blindness.

Saturday morning dawned. Kelly lounged in bed longer than usual, exhausted after last night's housework. By the time she'd come home on Friday afternoon someone had trimmed the tree and removed the fallen branch, and also replaced the blue tarp with a new picture window.

A man from a local furniture store had also appeared after supper and carted off the damaged sofa, promising her a replacement after the Independence Day holiday.

Considering the whole town had experienced similar problems, it was remarkable how her damage had received immediate attention. Obviously Ben had called in a few favors.

In any event, she'd spent the evening cleaning the living room from top to bottom, vacuuming the wall-to-wall carpeting over and over until she was convinced she had found every sliver of glass.

Carlie sat in front of the television, engrossed in cartoons. Taking advantage of her daughter's diverted at-

tention, Kelly unloaded her folder of accounting print-
outs and began to study the figures Vanessa had reluctantly furnished.

The amount of supplies didn't seem exorbitant. Based
on her work several years ago in establishing a clinic
lab, she thought the prices might be a little high. On the
other hand, her own paycheck didn't stretch as far as it
used to so perhaps inflation was responsible.

Coming to a quick decision, she dialed Mariah
Henning Prescott, her superior at TLC, Inc, hoping to
catch her at home.

'I have a favor to ask,' she told Mariah, after they'd
progressed past the usual exchange of personal gossip.

'Name it,' Mariah said.

'I wondered if I could locate a price list from several
other vendors. I think we're being overcharged for our
supplies.'

'I'll see what I can do,' Mariah promised. 'Want me
to mail or fax it to you?'

'Fax it,' Kelly answered, reciting the number.

Mariah repeated it. 'How's Carlie doing?'

'OK, I guess. Any news for me?'

Mariah's voice was apologetic. 'Sorry. Nothing permanent, I'm afraid. But I'm really pushing your résumé.'

'Thanks.'

'Have you decided what you'll do if I can't find the
type of job you're looking for?'

'No.' She'd pushed the dilemma from her mind, hoping the problem would solve itself. Yet it hadn't. Being
the first part of July, August was right around the corner.
The school term would begin soon too.

'I'm sure something will come along,' she said, injecting an optimistic note in her voice. 'Things always
work out.' She forced a chuckle. 'I may have to move

to some remote part of Alaska, but I'll find something so I can keep Carlie.'

'That's the spirit,' Mariah said. 'Don't give up yet. I'll be in touch.'

Kelly said her goodbyes, then stared at the work spread over the kitchen table. She had reached an impasse until the information arrived so she gathered the pages into a neat pile.

The doorbell rang unexpectedly.

Carlie's feet pounded across the floor as she ran to greet their visitor. 'It's Dr Ben!' she shouted.

Kelly glanced at the clock. Eleven a.m. and both she and Carlie were still wearing their sleeping attire. Her hair was tousled and her face devoid of make-up—not a way to dazzle a man, she thought. Especially not the man she wanted to impress.

Before she could sprint to the bedroom Ben's frame filled the doorway. He wore casual clothes—faded blue jeans and an open-necked hunter-green shirt.

'I came by to ask if you were ready to visit the horses,' he said, 'but I see you're not.'

His slow, thoroughly masculine perusal sent heat surging through her entire body. Her white satin nightgown covered her down to her toes, but the wisps of lace forming the bodice were intended for a man's pleasure. How did he always manage to catch her in nightclothes?

Fighting the urge to cover her breasts, her face flamed. 'It's Saturday. We like to sleep late.' She wrinkled her forehead in thought. 'How did you know we were going to Lewis's ranch today?'

Ben shrugged. 'He told me about his colts during his last appointment. I wanted to see them too so I thought we'd go together, have lunch and make a day of it.'

'Lunch?' He wanted to spend the *day* with them? She couldn't believe what she'd just heard.

He grinned. 'You know the meal between breakfast and dinner? It *is* eleven,' he pointed out. 'By the time you're ready it will be close to noon so I suggest you hurry.'

Nonplussed by the turn of events, she brushed past him to tell Carlie of the change in plans. Ben's hand shot out to stop her as she walked by.

'You don't mind if I go along, do you?'

The prospect of spending hours with him was too exciting to put into mere words. It seemed like a dream come true. And yet she was afraid for Carlie. She didn't want her to become attached to Ben, thinking he'd always be a part of their lives when he wouldn't.

However, she couldn't begrudge her daughter the opportunity to bask in male attention. Perhaps the two of them could show Ben exactly what he was missing because of his self-imposed exile, changing his attitude in the process.

'No. I don't mind,' she replied.

Something flashed in his eyes—a look of relief, perhaps—before his grin widened. 'Well, then,' he said, his bass voice parodying John Wayne's drawl, 'get a move on, missy. You're wastin' daylight.'

Both she and Carlie dressed in record time. She wore a pair of denim cut-offs and a red plaid shirt, while Carlie wore a black and white polka-dotted shorts set— her favorite because it reminded her of a Dalmatian's spots.

'Why don't I throw a few things together for a picnic?' Kelly volunteered as she re-entered the kitchen.

'Too late,' Ben said. 'It's out in the truck, provided Percy's kept his nose out of the basket. The July Fourth holiday may not be until tomorrow but we can celebrate it today.'

Carlie stood in the doorway, looking puzzled. 'But if

Mommy didn't cook, and we're having a picnic, doesn't that make it Mother's Day?'

Ben picked her up and settled her against his chest so her face was level with his. 'You bet. Do you like fireworks?'

Carlie's head bounced up and down and her eyes filled with expectation.

'Then we'll shoot a few sparkly things this evening to make your mommy's day more special,' Ben said. 'OK?'

Carlie's smile stretched from ear to ear and, clearly impatient, she bounced in his arms. 'Hurry up, Mommy. We're ready to go.'

Infected by her daughter's enthusiasm, Kelly grabbed an artist's pad and a box of charcoal pencils on her way to the door as she followed behind. It had been weeks since she'd had time to draw—not since they'd moved to Sundance—and her fingers itched to sketch this beautiful afternoon.

The Bateman ranch was fifteen miles north of town. Kelly enjoyed the drive, although the cab was cramped with two adults, a child and a large Dalmatian. The closer they got the more excited Carlie became.

'Mommy? Can we ride the colts?'

Kelly shook her head. 'They're just babies. They're not strong enough to carry you.'

'Oh. What about when they're older? Can I ride them then?'

How could she explain that their future was too uncertain to be making promises?

'We'll see,' Kelly answered.

A few minutes later Ben drove onto a road leading to the Bateman ranch and parked under a tree near the clapboard house. Lewis strode out of the barn on the east side of the property and waved in greeting as he approached.

'How-do, folks,' he called.

Kelly helped Carlie jump onto the gravel driveway. 'Hi, Lewis.'

'This must be young Carlie,' Lewis said, reaching out to ruffle the child's hair.

Carlie slipped behind Kelly, allowing her mother and Percy to form a shield. Lewis laughed at her shyness.

'Ready to see the horses?' he asked. As Carlie bobbed her head he crooked his finger at her. 'Come on. They're still in the barn.'

The group followed. Kelly noticed how Percy paired himself with Carlie rather with than his master. Ben fell into step beside Kelly, shortening his stride to match hers. It felt like the family outing Kelly had always wanted her daughter to experience. She memorized the details, eager to draw them as part of Carlie's living history.

A mixture of odors surrounded her as they entered the barn. Horse and cow, hay, alfalfa and grain scents mingled in a familiar combination. Lewis ushered them to a far stall where a mare munched happily on oats while two brown colts nuzzled her for their own meal.

Carlie poked her head through the fence planks to study them while Percy sat on his haunches beside her. 'They're so pretty,' she crooned. 'Look, Mommy! One of them's got a white spot on his forehead.' She giggled. 'And they both got socks on their feet.'

Kelly ignored her bad grammar. 'Yes, they do.'

'Did you give them names?' Carlie asked Lewis.

'Starfire and Stardust.' He grinned. 'My granddaughter picked those out once she heard Morning Star had twins.'

'How appropriate,' Kelly answered.

The colts, having noisily eaten their fill, staggered to the fresh straw and plopped down for a nap. 'Aren't they going to play?' Carlie asked, clearly disappointed.

'Probably later,' Ben said. 'We'll eat our lunch, and by the time we're finished they'll be ready to strut their stuff just for you.'

Lewis herded them toward the door. 'Our picnic spot is over there.' He pointed towards two large trees some fifty yards away. Their combined shade fell across a red-wood picnic table and its attached benches. 'Have fun.'

He left, leaving Kelly somewhat bewildered by, and suspicious of, his abrupt departure. Remembering Lewis's questions about her personal life, she wondered if he was trying to play Cupid. 'What's going on? How did he know we were having a picnic?'

Ben's complexion turned a ruddy hue as he led their small group toward his vehicle. 'I arranged it last night.'

'You did? What if I'd made other plans?'

He grinned. 'I gambled on you two joining me.'

The thought warmed her heart. 'I'm glad you did.'

Ben lifted an ice chest out of the back of his truck. 'Can you grab the basket for me?'

She did, peering into the container at the same time. He'd packed paper plates, napkins, silverware, a table-cloth and a blanket. He'd also tucked a tube of sunscreen and a can of insect repellent in one corner, indicating he'd planned this adventure thoroughly.

'I'm impressed. You've prepared well,' Kelly commented, snatching up her art supplies before following him across the yard. Carlie and Percy raced ahead.

'I tried,' he said.

As soon as Ben lowered the chest onto the bench Carlie tapped his arm. 'Percy wants to play fetch.'

'He does?'

Her curls bounced as she nodded.

'I should help your mother.'

'Go ahead,' Kelly said, as she covered the table with the red-checkered cloth. 'Setting out the food is the least I can do.'

Apparently convinced, he glanced down at Carlie. 'We need a sturdy stick.'

She brandished one from behind her back. 'Like this?'

'Perfect.'

Man, child and dog ambled into the open space. Ben sent the twig sailing into the distance and Percy raced after it, catching it between his teeth in mid-air.

Carlie jumped up and down with delight. 'Do it again,' she demanded, as Percy bounded back to his master with his prize.

Ben handed her the stick. 'You try.'

She pulled back her arm and, with a screwed-up expression on her face, threw with all her might. Once again the Dalmatian retrieved the prize, returning it to Carlie.

'My turn,' Ben said.

Carlie giggled and raced away. 'Got to catch me first.'

'I do, do I?' he teased, running after her.

Kelly watched him adjust his speed in order to remain two steps behind Carlie. Finally, he snatched her off the ground and lifted her high in the sky, before pretending to drop her. Carlie screamed with delight. Percy's woof added to the din.

Kelly clutched the paper plates to her chest, indelibly etching every minute detail on her memory. She'd never forget this scene as long as she lived.

She watched the sight for several minutes, unable to tear her gaze away. Ben had brought her daughter such joy and, from the look on his face, it was mutual.

She loved him for caring enough to play, for giving Carlie his undivided attention.

She loved him.

Her knees wobbled and she sank onto the bench, uncertain of her next move. Knowing how gun-shy he was at the thought of a relationship, if she told him how she felt he'd disappear from her life as quickly as he'd re-entered it. Her only choice was to wait. Perhaps, over time and under her tender loving care, he'd break free of his fears. Unfortunately, time was her enemy in more ways than one.

Ben's shout interrupted her train of thought. 'Is it ready to eat yet?'

Kelly jumped to her feet. 'Come and get it.' Pushing aside her worries, she opened the containers of chilled food and began serving.

The following hour passed swiftly. Carlie seemed extra-hungry, filling her plate to overflowing. Most of it, however, landed on the grass, rather than going into her stomach. Kelly wondered if Ben noticed how her daughter was supplementing Percy's diet.

The glance she exchanged with him over Carlie's head indicated that he had. 'You shouldn't give Percy any bones,' he cautioned Carlie. 'He might choke.'

'Oh.' Carlie placed the chicken wing she'd been dangling off the edge of the table onto her plate. Her plans obviously thwarted, she began to tear the meat from the bones, before dropping the bite-sized chunks into the eager Dalmatian's mouth.

'Don't forget to feed yourself,' Kelly said, 'otherwise you won't last until suppertime.'

At the end of their meal Kelly shooed Ben away to spread out the blanket while she stowed the leftovers in the cooler and bagged the trash.

Ben sat with his back against the tree trunk, stretching out his long legs and tucking his hands underneath his head. Percy, his tummy bulging, took up residence on one corner while Carlie stood close to Ben.

The ruffles of her outfit fluttered with her fidgety movements. 'Can we play fetch again?'

'In a while,' he answered promptly. 'If Percy runs now he'll get a stomach-ache.'

'Oh.' Carlie didn't argue, apparently concerned over Percy's health. She plopped down and scooted next to Ben, as if settling in for a long wait. He put one arm around her and drew her against his side, apparently not minding the child's chatter or her elbows digging into his ribs.

Touched by the scene, Kelly's breath caught and her throat burned with emotion. How could he possibly believe the things Alyce had told him? He *did* have enough of himself to spare for a family. To her, his actions proved it.

She sat at the table as she studied the scene. Flipping her pad to the next available page, she began to draw in smooth strokes.

'You're supposed to be resting,' he said.

'I am.' Kelly sketched the lines of his face, his high cheek-bones, his wind-blown hair. Once she'd created his likeness to her satisfaction she drew Carlie nestled against him with Percy and the tree in the background. Her pencil flew over the paper and she stopped only long enough to exchange it for a sharpened one.

Birds chirped overhead and a butterfly landed on the blanket. Percy studied the winged creature, then closed his eyes in total disinterest.

Fresh air carried a scent of grass and an occasional whiff of livestock. By the time she'd completed the drawing the sun had moved, shifting the light and lengthening the shade.

Carlie, Ben and Percy didn't move, fast asleep. Kelly

smiled as she turned the page. This time she drew from memory, choosing the scene in the barn with the mare and her colts.

Deep in her project, she didn't realize Ben had approached until he sat beside her, his forearm rubbing against hers. 'May I see?'

'Sure.' She tilted the book toward him, anxious for his opinion.

'You're really good.'

High praise indeed. 'Thanks.'

'I saw the sketch of Carlie in your living room. I didn't realize you were the artist.'

She smiled. 'I've framed a number of my drawings. I have as many pads as some people have photo albums. As far as I'm concerned, those are my treasures.'

Her work today would hold a very special place in her heart, more so if Carlie went to live with her grandparents. But she wisely kept that information to herself.

Percy lifted his head, obviously awakened by the sound of their voices. The next minute he stood up, walked closer to Carlie and sat on his haunches beside her. When she didn't stir he lay down.

Kelly motioned to Percy. 'He's a great babysitter.'

'I guess. I've never seen him this attentive.'

'Unfortunately, I don't know if her little Perdita will ever be a suitable substitute now that she's slept with the real thing,' she said wryly.

'So get her a dog.'

Kelly shook her head. 'It's hard enough, arranging for child care. It would be doubly difficult if a pet were involved.'

'So stop moving. It has to be tough, uprooting a child all the time.'

'Have you been talking to my mother?' she asked, hiding the guilt his words caused under levity.

'Just making an observation.'

'For your information, I'm hoping to settle in one place. A lot depends on the job market.'

'You could always get married.'

She pulled the pad closer and began drawing again. 'I could, but it wouldn't solve anything. Most families need two incomes these days.'

'So you don't want a husband?'

Kelly chewed on her lip, mentally framing a reply. If she disagreed he'd run for the proverbial hills. Yet she couldn't agree because she did want a spouse, albeit a very special one— one who would love her, cherish her and grant her freedom to make her own choices.

She answered in a half-truth. 'I haven't found anyone who meets my—or Carlie's—expectations.'

He turned to sit backwards, resting his forearms on the table behind him. His shirt strained across his pectoral muscles and she found it difficult to tear her gaze away.

'Ah. You're wanting someone to sweep you off your feet and take you to a world where you'll live happily ever after.'

'You don't have to be sarcastic about it,' she grumbled. 'Besides, you're wrong. I don't expect to be swept off my feet and I'm smart enough to know that happily ever after is only a fairy-tale.'

'Then what do you want?'

Kelly shrugged. 'Someone who'll treat me as an equal and treat Carlie as if she were his own daughter.' Someone who'd be willing to walk through fire for us, if necessary.

'Sounds reasonable. Why haven't you—?'

'Finding a person who meets both criteria is tough.'

His brow furrowed. 'I can't imagine anyone who wouldn't fall in love with Carlie.'

She rolled her eyes upwards. 'The men I've met don't want the responsibility. Most of them don't want to take care of their own children, much less someone else's.'

She winced, afraid he'd take her accusation personally. Wishing to recall her words, she stole a glance at him. He appeared thoughtful rather than wounded, and she was relieved.

'In any case, marriage isn't my top priority,' she continued lightly. 'Carlie and I are doing just fine on our own.'

'Speaking of Carlie,' he began, 'how did her lab work turn out?'

Kelly lowered her voice. 'All clear. No signs of infection.'

'Is she still having a problem?'

Thinking of the sheets waiting for attention, she sighed. 'Unfortunately, yes.'

'Our consulting urologist will have a clinic on Thursday. I'll work her into his schedule if you'd like.'

The thought of something inherently wrong causing the problem was frightening, but the sooner it was diagnosed the better. 'Thank you. I'd appreciate it.'

'Consider it done.' He stared into the brilliantly blue sky. Not a cloud was in sight. 'It's hard to believe we had such a bad storm a few days ago.'

'I know. By the way, I'm thrilled to have the window replaced. How did you manage to get the workmen to take care of it so quickly?'

He gave her a lazy grin. 'It pays to be a doctor in a small town. I'm a big fish in a little pond.'

Just as she'd suspected, everyone hurried to do his bidding. But it was nice to know that for once in her life she'd been the recipient of preferential treatment. 'Is that why you've never set up a practice in one of the larger communities?'

'No. I enjoy the variety of family-oriented medicine, although at times I wish we could deal with the more serious cases here. On the other hand, it would translate to a much heavier case-load, which isn't necessarily a good thing because we're busy enough as it is.'

Kelly understood. They were hard-pressed to handle the high volume of lab orders under current conditions.

'Besides, recruiting physicians to this part of the country isn't easy, and it wouldn't be economical to offer services that might be lost if one person pulled up his or her stakes. Our system of referrals works well. As a general rule, patients who don't make it after being transported wouldn't have survived anyway.'

'Speaking of transporting patients, how is Mr Cranston?'

'Stable, but serious. He underwent a splenectomy, but the nephrologist didn't think his kidneys suffered long-term damage. All things considered, he was a lucky man.'

'So was Gil Stephens, the snakebite case.' She shuddered. 'I utterly despise snakes of any kind. Carlie had better not ever want a pet snake because the answer will be no.'

Carlie sat up and yawned. 'What can't I have?' she asked, rubbing her eyes.

'A pet snake.'

'Oh. That's OK. I'd rather have dog like Percy.' She hugged the Dalmatian's neck.

Kelly grinned at Carlie's blatant hint. Suddenly she caught movement in her peripheral vision. 'Lewis must be going riding.'

Lewis led a spotted Appaloosa toward them. 'How's your picnic?' he called, as soon as he reached hearing distance.

'Wonderful,' Kelly answered.

He rubbed the horse's neck. 'I thought the young'un might be getting bored, so I saddled Betsy for her.'

Carlie's eyes grew wide. 'I can ride her?'

'Sure can.' He addressed Ben. 'I hate to leave you folks alone so much today, but one of my fences is down and I've got to fix it before my cattle take a notion to go visitin'.'

'Maybe we should leave,' Kelly suggested.

Lewis shook his head. 'Don't be silly. You're welcome to stay as long as you like. If I'm not back by the time you're finished with Betsy, Ben knows what to do with her tack.'

Lewis left and Ben swung Carlie into the saddle. 'Hold onto the horn,' he instructed, before speaking to Kelly. 'Want to walk along?'

She smiled. 'Go ahead. I'll wait here.'

Ben led the horse around the yard, disappearing behind a thicket. A few minutes later they trotted into view.

Ben was seated behind Carlie, holding her close to prevent her from being bounced out of the saddle.

Carlie wore a face-splitting smile and her high-pitched laughter filled the air. 'Faster,' she urged, giggling.

Ben's hearty chuckle touched Kelly's heart. 'I don't think so, scamp.'

The sight emphasized what Kelly had discovered a few hours earlier and what Carlie had instinctively known.

Ben was hero material.

If only she could convince him of his worth.

CHAPTER NINE

THE week passed. Carlie's appointment with the consulting urologist went fairly well. He'd reviewed the lab reports and performed a cystoscopy, which she didn't enjoy. However, Ben's unexpected arrival had redirected her attention during the uncomfortable procedure.

At last the examination was over. Kelly sent Carlie to play with the toys in the waiting room while Dr Rothman, a grandfatherly man in his late fifties, explained his findings.

'The good news is,' he began with a smile, 'that I didn't see anything unusual—no congenital anomalies or growths.'

Kelly's shoulders drooped in relief. Ben slipped her hand inside his and squeezed.

'On the other hand, I can't give you a physical explanation for her loss of control. It only happens at night, you say?'

Kelly nodded. 'She's never had trouble before, other than a few times when we first began toilet training.'

The men exchanged a glance, which didn't escape Kelly's notice. 'Do you suspect something else?' she asked, as fingers of fear began to tighten around her chest.

Dr Rothman crossed his arms. 'Dr Shepard and I will explore the possibility of other physical causes, but in the light of her history we have to consider a psychological origin.'

Kelly was stunned. 'Psychological?' she echoed.

Dr Rothman nodded. 'Did anything unusually stress-

ful occur about the time she began to wet the bed?
Perhaps difficulties with a babysitter, or a traumatic experience?'

Kelly's heart sank. Leaving Sheridan had been tough,
but she'd thought Carlie had adjusted to their new home.
Apparently her daughter's fears and insecurities had
manifested themselves in other ways.

'We moved to Sundance six weeks ago. She didn't
want to leave her friends behind.'

'Understandable,' he remarked. 'How is she coping?
Has she found any buddies yet?'

Her nod was half-hearted. Carlie didn't fuss and fume
about going to the day-care center any more and she
spoke often of Mary Beth and Lacey. However, she
hadn't invited any of her pals for a play session at home.

If Dr Rothman had noticed her weak response he
didn't comment. 'I'm sure the situation will eventually
resolve itself. In the meantime, try waking her up during
the night to use the bathroom. As another option you
can purchase an enuresis alarm for her bed.'

'I understand.' Although her instinct confirmed Dr
Rothman's diagnosis, something he'd said stuck in her
mind. 'You mentioned other physical causes.'

Dr Rothman cleared his throat. 'We've already ruled
out any infection, but sometimes undiagnosed diabetes
can be the culprit. I'll order a chemistry panel and a CBC
to check out her glucose level and her overall health. I
don't expect to find anything unusual, but it doesn't hurt
to be thorough.'

He addressed Ben. 'If you have any other concerns,
let me know.'

'I will,' Ben answered.

The urologist left the room for his next patient, leaving Ben and Kelly alone.

'I hear the fish are biting,' he commented. 'Shall we check it out tonight?'

The idea was tempting, but in view of Dr Rothman's assessment she tempered her refusal with an apologetic smile. 'I don't think so. Carlie and I need to discuss a few things, make a few decisions.'

'Like becoming part of a community, rather than drifting in and out?'

'Yes. I put in my application for the new position but if I don't get it I'll have to—' Her voice caught in her throat. 'My parents want Carlie to live with them so she can start school. They've been asking about it for a long time.'

'I won't live at Grandma's without you,' Carlie cried from the doorway, tears streaming down her face. 'I won't! I won't!'

Kelly turned at the sound of her daughter's voice. How long had she been listening? 'I don't want you to either,' she soothed, crouching to Carlie's level and hugging her, 'but we may not have a choice.'

'Please, Mommy, don't leave me there.' Carlie looked up at Ben. 'Please, Dr Ben. Don't let my mommy go away and leave me.'

Before Ben could reply Kelly wiped away the moisture on Carlie's face. 'It isn't up to Ben. This is something that you and I have to work out for ourselves. Let's go home.' Rising, she grabbed Carlie's hand and headed for the hallway.

Carlie stumbled along behind, staring over her shoulder at Ben as if he were her savior. It pained Kelly to see how Carlie expected Ben, rather than her own mother, to solve her dilemma.

She glanced at him. To her surprise, he appeared lost in unhappy thoughts so she left, without interrupting.

Carlie didn't say a word during the drive home and

Kelly thought it best. This was too volatile a discussion to begin when she needed to focus on the road.

As soon as she'd parked the van Carlie went directly to her room. Deciding she, too, needed a few minutes alone, Kelly prepared supper. As soon as she'd shoved the tuna casserole into the oven she knocked on Carlie's door.

'May I come in?' she asked.

For a long minute nothing happened. Finally, the knob turned and the door opened. Carlie hopped back on the bed and lay down, staring at the ceiling.

Kelly sat beside her. For several minutes she didn't say anything, waiting for Carlie's outburst. When Carlie did speak her voice was hardly audible.

'Grandma said there would be a time when you would go away.'

Anger began to build in Kelly's chest. No wonder Carlie exhibited signs of stress. 'She did? When?'

Carlie shrugged. 'After we moved here.'

Kelly remembered the call. She'd passed the phone to Carlie and had gone to the bathroom to calm down. Now that she thought about it, Carlie's problems had begun a few days later.

'Grandpa said I could live at their house while you went to work. I said that I didn't want to live there unless you did too.'

'And what did he say?' Kelly coaxed.

'Grandma said that if we had to be apart it would be OK because I was a big girl now. You would visit me as often as you could. To keep me from being lonely, they'd buy me my very own pony.'

A lump clogged Kelly's throat. How could her parents do this to their granddaughter and to *her*? Surely they knew how burdened any five-year-old would be at the idea of her mother leaving her on her grandparents' doorstep like an unwanted package.

Carlie sniffled and wiped her nose with the back of her hand. 'I don't wanna be a big girl, Mommy.'

The plaintive note brought tears to Kelly's eyes and a sharp pain to her chest. 'Is that why you started having accidents? You didn't want to be a big girl?'

Carlie sat up and flung her arms around Kelly's neck, holding on for dear life. 'Please, Mommy. Don't send me away. I promise I won't do it again. Ever.'

Kelly clutched Carlie's body close. Breathing in her sweet child scent, she berated herself for putting Carlie—and herself—in this situation.

'I don't want to send you to live with Grandma and Grandpa. I want you to live with me. Don't ever forget it.'

'Then I won't have to?' Carlie asked.

Kelly hesitated, trying to explain their uncertain future so Carlie would understand. 'I'll do everything I can so it *won't* happen. I didn't mention Grandma's idea before because if my job in Sundance turned into a permanent one then everything would be solved. If it didn't I planned to talk this over with you before we made any decisions on where we'd live.'

'I don't like Grandma's idea, Mommy.'

Kelly tried to placate her. 'I don't either, but school will start in a couple of weeks. Grandma and Grandpa—and I—thought it would be better if you stayed in one place. We know how much it upsets you to find new friends.'

Although she intended to exchange a few choice words with her parents she didn't want to alienate them from Carlie. They were, after all, Carlie's only relatives who took an interest in her life.

'But can't *we* stop moving?' Carlie asked. 'Mary

Lou's mom works at the li-berry and she doesn't have to move at all. You could work there too.'

Kelly smoothed Carlie's hair as she smiled. 'But I'm not a librarian. I know it's hard, but be patient.'

Carlie scooted back against the headboard and crossed her arms. A familiar stubbornness appeared on her face. 'I won't go to school until then. I don't want to live with Grandma and Grandpa.'

Hoping to divert her, Kelly asked, 'You like learning things in pre-school. You can recite the alphabet and you know your numbers. Why, you can even print your name. You don't want to miss out on reading and addition and all those things, do you?'

Carlie screwed up her face in obvious consideration. 'I will,' she said solemnly, 'so we can be together.'

Kelly sent up a silent prayer for patience. Carlie's wall of resistance showed no signs of cracking. Even so, her daughter's willingness to give up the one thing she'd anticipated for the past year touched her heart.

'Like I said, we're probably worrying for nothing. If you *did* have to stay with Grandma and Grandpa, I promise it wouldn't be for long.'

Carlie's mouth formed a pout. 'How long?'

'A few weeks. Just until I find the right place for us. We've seen a lot of nice towns in our travels. Would you like to go back to any of them? How about Sheridan or Casper or—?'

'I wanna live in Sundance. I love Dr Ben and Percy and I don't want to leave 'em. Can we stay?' Carlie begged.

Kelly drew a bracing breath. 'I'd like that too, but we don't always get what we want,' she said gently.

Carlie rubbed her eyes and sniffled. 'I'm gonna really, really, really, miss Percy and Dr Ben.'

'I know,' Kelly whispered, her voice failing her. 'We

have a few more weeks so try not to worry about it, OK? If we move away we'll come back for a visit.'

'It won't be the same, though. Percy might forget me.'

And Ben might forget me, Kelly thought. 'Don't be so sure. Percy likes you a lot. He'll remember you.' She rose. 'Come on. Time for supper.'

Normally their meals were cheerful affairs. Today, however, Carlie spoke little, toying with her food instead of eating it. Kelly tried to coax Carlie out of her doldrums, but failed. Her own spirits were low, drained by their intense discussion.

The doorbell rang. Instead of dashing to greet their visitor, Carlie remained seated.

'Why don't you see who it is?' Kelly urged.

Carlie's fork clattered onto her plate before she trudged into the other room. 'It's Dr Ben,' she said without enthusiasm. Kelly rose to stand in the connecting doorway.

'Hi, half-pint,' Ben said. 'I wondered if you wanted to go fishing.'

'I don't think so,' Carlie said.

Ben stroked his chin. 'Hmm. That's too bad. I found some nice fat, juicy worms.'

Carlie sighed and her shoulders drooped. 'I don't feel like fishing tonight.'

Ben crouched down to child's-eye level. 'Are you sick?'

'No.'

'Is there something on your mind?' he asked.

She nodded. 'My mommy says I might have to live with my grandma and grandpa so I can go to school.'

'And you don't want to?' he asked.

Carlie shook her head vehemently. 'I want us to stay here with you and Percy.'

'That would be nice,' he agreed.

'Since you don't have a little girl at your house to play with Percy, could I be your little girl?'

Kelly tensed. Her fingernails dug into her palms as she waited for his reply.

'I had a little girl once. I wasn't a very good daddy.'

'Did you spank her?'

He smiled. 'No. I just wasn't around when she needed me because I was busy with my patients. You're a very special person. You deserve a very special father who'll look after you.'

Kelly closed her eyes to the pain in her chest. Ben had spent a part of every day with them since the storm. During that time her hopes had mushroomed with the prospect of changing his attitude. In five short seconds he'd smashed those hopes as thoroughly as the branch had destroyed her window.

If Ben Shepard was too cowardly to live in the present then she didn't want him around her daughter, making her wish for the fulfillment of obviously impossible dreams.

'You're special,' Carlie pointed out. 'You've always been here when we needed you.'

Out of the mouths of babes... Kelly took that moment to interrupt. 'I think Percy would like to play.'

'OK.' Her conversation apparently not as interesting as a romp with Percy, she hurried outside.

Ben rose. 'So you told her the situation?'

Kelly returned to the kitchen, hiding her frustration as she cleared away the supper neither of them had enjoyed.

'Yes. I explained how living with her grandparents was a possibility, not a certainty. If it comes to pass....at least she's been forewarned.'

'When will you know?'

Kelly scraped the leftovers into the garbage disposal. 'Some time during this next month before my contract ends. If I'm lucky, Ed will hire me to fill his position. Mariah, my boss, has been checking around too. If she doesn't find any openings I'll figure out something else.'

'I'll put in a good word—'

'No.' Her response was vehement. 'I want this job based on my own merits, not because someone—you— pulled a few strings.'

He fell silent. 'Are you sure?'

'Absolutely.' She'd never prove her independence if she allowed him to rescue her every time she had a problem. She refused to have him lump her in the same category as his ex-wife.

Her wounds too fresh to continue the conversation, she changed the subject. 'As you can see, neither of us are in the mood for an excursion this evening. You'll have to find another fishing partner.' She brushed past him on her way to wash off the table.

He snagged her arm. 'You're upset.'

'Shouldn't I be? I'm angry with my parents for jumping the gun and worrying Carlie, without giving her all the details. I'm angry with myself for not discussing the possibility before now. I'm angry with Carlie's father for deserting us and I'm angry with—' She cut herself off.

'Me,' he finished.

Kelly took a deep breath and met his piercing gaze. 'Yes, I am.'

'For telling her the truth?'

Amongst other things, she thought.

'I had to,' he continued, a trace of desperation in his voice. 'I couldn't let her consider me as a potential father. It wouldn't be fair.'

'I'm afraid you're too late—the damage has been done. The best thing for you to do is to stay away from

her. From us.' For the first time since her move to
Sundance she didn't want Ed to hire her. She didn't want
to see Ben on a daily basis, knowing they only had a
platonic future ahead of them.

And yet, if this was the place for them to put down
roots, she'd grit her teeth and bear it. After all, Carlie's
well-being was the issue, not hers.

'I tried,' he said, his smile wan. 'Unfortunately, I can't
seem to do it. Regardless, I realized something today.
I'd let Alyce take Tanya away from me, just like your
parents are trying to take Carlie.'

'Yes, I suppose they are,' she said. 'I never thought
of it quite like that.'

'Please don't do what I did. Don't give in without a
fight or let them emotionally blackmail you. I'd always
wanted my daughter, but I truly believed Alyce's assessment of my character. Alyce took advantage of my
guilt and convinced me that letting Tanya go would be
in her best interests.'

Kelly saw the parallels. Her parents were playing on
her guilt to obtain what *they* wanted, not what Carlie or
Kelly wanted.

'In any case, I came by to encourage you to hang onto
your daughter, by whatever means necessary.'

'I intend to,' she said fiercely.

His hand dropped. 'I also wanted to tell you that I'll
be gone the week after next. I'm scheduled to attend a
conference in Cheyenne after the first of the month.'

'August isn't far off,' she said. Although only a minute ago she'd told him to stay away, deep down she
didn't want it to happen.

'I'll miss you.'

Those last three words melted her anger toward him.
'I'll miss you too.'

Without warning, his hand cupped the back of her

head, pulling her closer as he lowered his mouth to hers. His kiss was intense, demanding and unrestrained.

This was no gentle peck. It was a kiss of power, of passion, of a man who spoke his feelings not by words but by his deeds.

Her arms circled his neck. Somehow her feet left the floor as if she were weightless. She certainly felt so. Her inner ache burst into full bloom and she craved a fulfillment she'd never experienced.

Her breasts flattened against his chest. His hands caressed her back before he pressed her pelvis to his in a way that left no question as to the aroused state of his body.

A playful bark drifted in through the open window, reminding her of the time and place. 'We can't do this,' she muttered. 'Carlie...'

He shuddered, then sighed as he lowered her to the floor with obvious reluctance. 'You're right.'

Kelly retreated to the sink, readjusting her clothing as she did so.

'If you stay in Sundance, and I'm sure you will, I'd like to help you find a house.'

Hadn't he heard a word she'd said? Just because she'd had a moment of weakness and kissed him didn't mean the issues were resolved.

'Why?' she asked bluntly. 'If you don't want to raise Carlie's hopes don't torture her, by hanging around.' Or me either, she finished silently. 'You're not interested in hearth and home and I'm not in the market for an affair.'

He hesitated. 'I just want to be sure no one takes advantage of you. Also, I want you to have a nice home in a good neighborhood where Carlie will be safe.'

'Sundance is a safe town,' she said. 'I'm sure we'll be fine wherever we choose to live. As for being taken advantage of, I've been on my own for the last six years. I'm not as naïve as you think.'

How could she ever make him understand that the perfect place was with him? Couldn't he see that his worry over Carlie signaled more than polite concern? What would it take for his head to stop fighting his heart?

She drew a deep breath. 'In any case, if and when I need to start house-hunting I'll take care of it myself. Where we live is my responsibility, not yours. Now, if you don't mind, it's getting late and Carlie needs her bath.'

Looking thoughtful, he ambled toward the door.

'Have a good time at your conference,' she said. Perhaps he'd catch her hint that she didn't intend or expect to see him beforehand.

'Thanks.' He stepped outside and called for Percy.

Within minutes, his truck rolled down the driveway and out of sight.

The pain of him leaving hurt Kelly far more than she'd ever dreamed. She hadn't even felt such a horrific sense of loss when Slade had fled to his greener pastures.

Later, after she'd tucked Carlie into bed and read three fairy-tales of princes rescuing princesses, she retreated to the living room and sat in the dark.

If Ben wanted to isolate himself from a future with her and Carlie, then so be it. She didn't intend to do the same. She wanted to right the wrongs in her life, to seize a second chance at having a hero of her own. Waiting for Ben to realize his potential was foolhardy. He *was* capable of managing his practice and having a personal life—he'd shown that repeatedly over the past few weeks.

Unfortunately, if she hadn't convinced him of that by now she never would.

Accepting her loss was her only course of action. No more visits to Lewis's ranch with Ben, no more picnics, no more asking for assistance even if the house fell down around her ears.

Ben's absence would be difficult for Carlie but, given time, she would be forced to accept the inevitable.

Ben Shepard would never receive what they had to offer until he stopped carrying guilt in his heart and made room for them instead.

After a week of studying the purchasing print-outs in every moment of her spare time, Kelly's spirits had dropped to an all-time low. She'd hoped to find a large mark-up in the contracting company's prices but, according to the list Mariah had faxed her, their fees compared to those of their competitors.

Feeling pressured because the due date of her report was approaching fast, she reluctantly turned over the files she'd received from the materials management department.

'Was everything in order?' Vanessa smirked.

Kelly wished she could wipe the self-satisfied smile off the purchasing agent's face. 'As far as I could tell.'

'My staff and I know what we're doing. Don't forget it.'

'I won't. However, I still want to review all bills pertaining to our section before they're paid.'

Vanessa's eyes narrowed. 'I've allowed you your little investigation into this section's affairs, but enough is enough. When Ed returns I'll inform him—and others—that you repeatedly question my work.'

Although Vanessa was a formidable adversary—spiteful enough to cause problems for anyone who crossed her—Kelly refused to back down. 'I don't think he'll complain about a conscientious effort to watch our expenditure, do you?'

'You're here on sufferance,' Vanessa snapped. 'Do you honestly think you have any power to institute new policies?'

'Maybe, maybe not. However, I intend to do the best job I possibly can while I'm here.' Kelly strode out, her nerve endings quivering with suppressed emotion. She'd hoped to establish a congenial working relationship with the woman in order to exchange ideas, but Vanessa's snobbish attitude made it impossible. Unfortunately, Kelly had reached a brick wall and she didn't know a way to go around it.

She dreaded announcing her failure to Ed and the task force. More important, she could see the expression on Ben's face. His distaste over her inability to handle an assignment would be in plain view. Although his opinion shouldn't matter, it did.

'Hi, Kelly. How's it going?' Vern fell into step beside her.

Kelly glanced at the X-ray tech who'd broken her concentration.

'Same stuff, different day,' she said, responding to his happy-go-lucky manner. 'You know how it is.'

'I'm taking my niece on a trail ride this weekend. Would you and your daughter like to join us?'

She started to refuse, but her side vision captured a glimpse of Ben as he rounded the far corner on his way to the ER. Just because he didn't want commitment didn't mean she couldn't accept other invitations. 'Yeah. Sure. Why not?'

'Great. I'll pick you up around nine. See you then.'

Vern walked away. Her view unblocked, she noticed a frown on Ben's face as he, too, disappeared from view. Before she could mull over the situation a young woman she'd seen working in the business office approached, carrying an armload of inter-office mail.

'I'm so glad our paths crossed,' Celia said in her anxious-to-please voice. 'I was on my way to deliver this, but if you wouldn't mind taking it now it would save me a few steps.'

Kelly took the brown envelope. 'Sure. Anything important?'

'Invoices for you to review before I issue payment. Just like you'd asked.'

Although Vanessa had threatened to stop Kelly's pilot project, she'd obviously not done so as yet. Kelly decided not to draw attention to the fact. The more she discovered before Ed returned from his latest round of testing at Rapid City the better she could withstand Vanessa's accusations.

'Thanks. I'll bring these back by the end of the day. Tomorrow at the latest.'

'Take your time.'

They parted company. Kelly opened the envelope as she ambled toward the lab. Four packing slips were affixed to their respective invoices. The fifth one, however, was alone.

Pondering why the invoice didn't have a matching packing slip, indicating the shipped goods, she glanced at the letterhead.

Global Medical Supply.

She was familiar with the major companies so Global Medical was either a small, independent firm, trying to gain a foothold in the healthcare market, or it didn't carry laboratory products. Perhaps one of the other services conducted business with them and their bill had landed in her pile by accident.

A new idea popped into her head. Was her department spending their budgeted dollars paying for another area's materials? Excited at the possible explanation, she hurried back to her area.

'Guess what?' she told Dee. 'I may have found something.'

Dee looked up from the chemistry analyzer's computer terminal. 'What?'

Kelly waved the offending piece of paper under Dee's nose. 'Global Medical Supply. What do we purchase from them?'

Dee's brow wrinkled in thought. 'Nothing that I know of. I don't recognize the name.'

'Neither do I. I think the lab's budget is excessively high because we're paying someone else's bills.'

'Well, hey, that's good news. But which section's?'

Kelly frowned. 'I don't know. But I intend to find out.' She telephoned Celia and posed her question.

'To be honest, I couldn't say,' Celia said. 'In all the years I've written the checks I've never seen a packing list.'

Kelly was stumped by the obvious breach in policy and procedure. 'Isn't that unusual?'

'Yes, but the first few times Purchasing always attached a note, authorizing payment. I discussed it with my boss and he said to write the checks. I have ever since.'

'Who authorized it in Purchasing?'

'Vanessa.'

The whole thing smelled as nasty as a culture plate of salmonella in its hydrogen sulfide-producing glory. Kelly intended to research good old Global Medical Supply on her own.

If she had stumbled across something shady, asking questions around the hospital might inadvertently alert the guilty party and give them an opportunity to cover his or her tracks.

'I wish I had Internet access,' she told Dee.

'The public library's on-line.'

'Great. I'll go there.' Kelly's excitement grew. She couldn't wait until the end of her shift to pick up Carlie and begin her self-appointed project.

For the rest of the afternoon she tore through Ed's entire bookcase of lab supplier catalogs in search of Global Medical and came up empty.

At the library she began one Yellow Pages search after another, branching into international circles as well. After exhausting all avenues, she came to one conclusion.

Global Medical Supply didn't exist.

CHAPTER TEN

'Now what?' Ben snapped as he walked into ER, after seeing Kelly in the hallway.

Cheryl handed him a clipboard. 'Grumpy, are we?'

He didn't answer. The nurse had accurately identified his symptoms, but only he knew the diagnosis—jealousy. The thought of Vern taking Kelly and Carlie on an outing burned like acid in his gut. Yet he couldn't fault her for not refusing—he'd certainly made it clear that he wasn't willing to exchange his solitary lifestyle for one of permanent companionship.

He gritted his teeth as he forced his feelings aside with a great deal of effort. This was a perfect example of how personal affairs distracted his professional concentration.

He waved the clipboard. 'Where is she?'

Cheryl pointed to the over-sized numeral scrawled in the top right-hand corner. 'Room two.'

Chagrined, Ben ignored her Cheshire-cat smile. 'What did Allen find?'

'Textbook case of acute mountain sickness. Headache, drowsiness, dizziness, nausea and vomiting, facial pallor. She and her friend were hiking on Sundance Mountain when she started feeling ill. Claims she hasn't felt good since she arrived.'

Ben didn't look away from the notes. 'Where does she live?'

'Alabama.'

He tried to pass the clipboard back to Cheryl. 'I agree with Allen's diagnosis.'

Cheryl refused to take it. 'Fine, but Ms Abernathy

wants a second opinion. She's convinced that she couldn't *possibly* suffer from altitude sickness since she's in such *excellent* physical condition.' Cheryl mimicked a southern drawl as she spoke. 'She works out *faithfully* at a health club, you know.'

Ben gave her a parody of a salute, before entering room two with Cheryl accompanying him. Inside he found two women, both blondes and both possessing figures which qualified them to pose for *Sports Illustrated*'s Swimsuit edition.

His patient was obviously the one sitting on the bed, rubbing her temples. 'Ms Abernathy?' he asked.

She glanced at him. 'Yes.' Her accent came through loud and clear with only the one word.

'I'm Dr Shepard. I'm here to review your case.'

'That's wonderful. I just can't believe that I could possibly suffer from mountain sickness. My fitness level is extremely high.'

'When did you begin your climb in relation to your arrival?' he asked.

'Let's see. We flew into Rapid City on the red-eye flight this morning, rented a car and here we are.' Her hands fluttered helplessly.

'Take a deep breath, please,' Ben instructed, as he listened to her lung sounds. 'Didn't anyone warn you about acclimatizing yourself to the altitude, before beginning any strenuous activity?'

'Yeah, but the day was simply too gorgeous to spend sitting in a little ol' room.'

He stuffed the stethoscope into his trouser pocket. 'You haven't given yourself enough time to adjust to the altitude.'

'Why am I sick and Millicent isn't?' Rhea pronounced 'I' as 'ah'.

'She apparently has a greater tolerance for hypoxia—

a fancy word for reduced oxygen in the tissues. Don't worry. If you take things easy you should be through the worst of it in the next twenty-four to forty-eight hours.'

'Look at the bright side, Rhea,' Millicent interjected. 'We'll relax at the lodge and find those two delicious-looking fellows who offered to buy us a drink.'

'No alcohol,' Ben ordered. 'No smoking either.'

Rhea gave him a decided pout of her full lips. 'Not even one teensy, weensy mint julep?'

Behind him, Cheryl smothered a cough.

'Not even a sip,' Ben said firmly. 'I'll give you a prescription for acetazolamide, which will help your symptoms. Take one pill every twelve hours. I also want to administer oxygen before you leave. Any questions?'

'Not at the moment, sugar,' Rhea said.

Ben turned to Cheryl. 'Give her two to three liters per minute of oxygen. As soon as she feels perky she's free to leave.'

Cheryl nodded. Ben left the small cubicle, anxious to complete his notes. By the time he'd finished Cheryl had joined him at the desk.

'That woman is positively nauseating,' she declared, rummaging in the desk for a new pen. 'If she says one more word about how she has such trouble finding clothes to fit her figure, I'm going to be sick. So I don't have a nineteen-inch waist. I'd like to see how she'll look after she's had three kids.'

Muttering about the unfairness of life, she stomped towards room two and the southern belle.

Unbidden, a mental picture of Kelly appeared to Ben. He visualized how she must have looked when she was pregnant with Carlie, how she'd look if she were swollen with his child.

He tipped his chair back and allowed his imagination

free rein. Carlie would, no doubt, be a most helpful—and most attentive—older sister.

The smile on his face died as he replayed the scene he'd witnessed between Kelly and Vern. Kelly was like a vintage Corvette, something he wanted but couldn't afford. Perhaps by the time he'd returned from his conference he'd be back to normal.

Mariah phoned Kelly on Wednesday. 'I've looked high and low for Global Medical ever since you called. I even contacted a friend of mine at American Hospital Supply and they've never heard of it.'

'It's a dummy company?' Kelly asked, her heart pounding with excitement.

'As far as we can tell,' Mariah agreed. 'The only question is who started it?'

'I have an idea,' Kelly said, her mind focusing on the obvious choice. 'Proving it is my only problem.'

'If I can do anything else, let me know.'

'I will,' Kelly promised. 'You've already been a big help.'

'Unfortunately, not big enough,' Mariah said, her tone apologetic. 'I have a ton of temporary jobs available, but permanent positions are scarce. Too many places are downsizing and only want extra staff during their peak times. I'm sorry.'

Fierce disappointment swept over Kelly. 'Thanks for trying. Keep me posted.'

After disconnecting the call, she dialed Ben's office. She'd investigated the money issue as far as she could. Now it was time to turn over the information to someone who possessed enough authority to act on it.

'I'm sorry, but Dr Shepard's out of town,' the receptionist revealed.

'He is? I thought he wasn't leaving for his conference until Sunday.'

'Those were his original plans, but he changed them unexpectedly.'

'I see.'

'Shall I leave a message? If it's a medical problem Dr Powell is covering.'

'No. No message.' Kelly numbly replaced the receiver as a sense of loss gripped her in its icy embrace. She shouldn't care if he didn't include her in his plans, she scolded herself. His life was his own—she didn't have a part in it.

Deep in the throes of her personal agony, she didn't notice Dee and Don Jamison, the human resources director, standing outside Ed's office until her colleague knocked on the door.

'Kelly?' Dee asked brightly. 'Don is looking for you.'

Hoping for good news, she welcomed him into Ed's office. Behind Don's back Dee gave her a thumbs-up sign before she walked away.

Don, however, remained standing. 'You'll receive a letter in the mail, but I thought I should tell you the news in person.' He hesitated. 'We've selected another candidate.'

Her world collapsed. 'I see.'

'One of our local boys wants to come home,' Don said. 'He just finished school and took his registry exam. You can understand our dilemma.'

Kelly struggled to keep her voice even. 'Of course. When will he start?'

'Monday. So after next week we won't need you.'

Curiosity compelled her to ask, 'When did Ed make the decision? He's been gone for the past week.'

He appeared uncomfortable. 'He didn't, actually. As soon as I received Lane's application those of us on Ed's selection committee met. We simply felt safer in choosing someone who has ties to the community. In addition, we couldn't afford to pay you a salary commensurate with your experience. I'm sorry.'

She squared her shoulders and pasted a smile on her face. 'Thanks for being honest.'

He ambled towards the door. 'If we ever need temporary services again we'll request you.'

'Thanks,' she repeated numbly. His praise brought little comfort.

As soon as Don left, her legs lost their stuffing and she leaned against Ed's desk. The doors in her life seemed to be slamming shut with a vengeance.

Dee rushed in a moment later. 'Well?' the older woman demanded.

'Your new person, Lane somebody or other, starts on Monday.'

Shock drove the color out of Dee's face. 'What?'

'Your new person—' Kelly began to repeat.

'No, no, no.' Dee waved her hands. 'What about *you*?'

'I'll stay the week and then I'm gone.'

The older woman perched on the edge of the nearest chair, plainly astonished. 'How could Ed *do* this?'

'He didn't. The committee met and decided they couldn't refuse to hire a local.'

'If this isn't a fine kettle of fish.' Dee stood straight and tall, appearing like an avenging angel in spite of her average height.

Kelly straightened. 'Yes, well, variety is the spice of life,' she said, trying to cheer herself as well as her colleague. 'I'm resilient.'

She'd weathered worse storms than this. Another one wouldn't matter. The only good thing was that the cloud of uncertainty no longer hung over her head. It was a time to make plans rather than drift along as she had for the past few weeks. She must be a slow learner. Only *she* could make her dreams come true. Wishing for the best was a futile exercise.

Energy surged through her. This was the perfect time to leave. With Ben out of town, Carlie wouldn't suffer through a tearful, stressful goodbye.

Neither would she. She wouldn't watch his arms enfold her daughter in a bear hug while she herself wished to be in the exact spot, breathing in his scent and drawing on his strength.

She wouldn't see Carlie plant a tearful kiss on his cheek while *she* wanted to taste his mouth one more time, feel the rasp of his whiskers against her cheek, enjoy his loving caress.

She wouldn't hear Carlie's cries of love when she wanted to shout her own feelings from the rooftops.

'In fact, I'll end my contract on Monday,' Kelly began, cementing her thoughts into a decision. 'After Lane arrives I'm extraneous.'

'You'll miss the county rodeo,' Dee wailed. 'Besides, don't you want to stay until Ben gets back?'

'No.' She didn't elaborate, holding her counsel even under the pressure of Dee's piercing gaze.

'I thought you and Ben would—'

'You were wrong.'

'You're running away.'

'I'm running toward my future,' Kelly corrected. 'Ben doesn't want one—at least not with us—because he's still tied to his past.'

'What about your report to the task force? I don't have the slightest idea how to finish it.'

Kelly smiled at Dee's utter dismay. 'I'll write it this weekend and turn it in on Monday.'

'That's a relief,' Dee said, sounding as if her faith in

Kelly hadn't been misplaced. 'What did you recommend?'

'For the hospital attorney to look into the possibility of fraud and embezzlement.'

Dee's eyes seemed to double in size. 'Good heavens! What *did* you find?'

'As far as I can tell, Vanessa authorizes payments to a company that doesn't exist.'

Dee's jaw dropped. 'You're kidding.'

Kelly shrugged. 'I wish I was. Celia sends the checks to a post office box in Nevada. I'm sure the money eventually surfaces in Vanessa's account.'

Dee whistled and Kelly continued. 'Unfortunately, I can't prove it without access to her bank records, which is why the legal authorities have to investigate.'

'No wonder Vanessa dug in her heels every time you asked to see any paperwork. She was apparently afraid you might stumble across something and expose her operation.'

'I'd say so.'

'You need to tell Ben. He should be here. This could make the national news!'

Kelly managed a wan smile. 'I intended to, but he left town early this morning. I'm on my own.'

'When he gets back—' Dee began.

'I'll be long gone.'

'Leave a message at his hotel. Today.'

'His conference doesn't start until Monday. I don't know where he went in the meantime.' Even if she'd known his whereabouts she would have refused to call him. Ben wanted someone independent, not someone who interrupted his meetings for instructions or advice.

'All I ask,' Kelly continued, 'is that you don't breathe a word of this to anyone. Vanessa will be thrilled to hear I'm leaving because she'll think her secret is still safe.

Whatever happens after the meeting will be the administrator's decision.'

'My lips are sealed.'

Kelly touched her colleague's arm. 'Hey, don't look so sad. It was great working with you while it lasted.'

'Where are you going next?' Dee asked. 'I'd like to keep in touch.'

Kelly rubbed at the tension in her neck. She'd stay at her parents' house for a few weeks and help Carlie adjust to the new surroundings. The thing she'd feared the most had come to pass.

'Hang onto your daughter, by whatever means necessary.' Ben's words drifted out of her memory as a conscious thought.

She couldn't give Carlie up so easily, could she?

No, she decided. Her profession was important, but not more so than her daughter. Perhaps it was time to pursue the graphic design classes she'd always wanted to take but had never had the chance.

If she was careful her savings account could last until she established herself in another career. It would mean postponing their dream of purchasing a home—complete with a yard and a Dalmatian—but, given the alternative, Carlie wouldn't object.

She could check out the colleges during the next few weeks and enroll for the fall session at the same time Carlie did. The more she considered this new option the more certain she felt that it was the right thing to do.

With any luck she'd be so busy that she wouldn't think of Benjamin Shepard and what might have been.

Ben strode into Cheyenne's convention hall on Monday morning and chose a seat near the back. Voices murmured around him like bees, scouting for the right place to land.

He glanced at the program. He'd looked forward to hearing the speakers at this medical symposium for months, but now, as he reviewed the schedule, the topics seemed dull.

Get a grip, he told himself. Of course he wanted to know the latest techniques in pain management, hear about the cutting-edge drugs to combat high cholesterol and hypertension, learn the newest cancer therapies.

He shifted in his seat, willing himself into enthusiasm. It was impossible. His thoughts drifted towards the events of the past few days.

After his last confrontation with Kelly he'd examined his life with a critical eye and had disliked what he'd seen. Cheryl's accusation had hit the mark. He'd isolated himself both emotionally and socially.

Hoping to find a way to reverse his direction, he'd taken several days of his accumulated vacation and had gone to visit his daughter in Denver.

Tanya had seemed glad to see him, telling him of her friends and the school activities she participated in with her thirteen-year-old friends.

Alyce had seemed much happier than he remembered her ever being. Either time had matured her or her new husband complemented her personality better than Ben had. It was probably a little of both.

In any case, Alyce had moved on with her life, adding a son to her family. She'd risen out of those dark days of their marriage, like a phoenix rising out of ashes.

He needed to do the same.

After securing a promise from Tanya to visit him before school started, he'd backtracked to Cheyenne. The crushing weight of guilt had lifted and he literally felt ten years younger.

His mind raced with plans, beginning with his return

to Sundance. He'd find Kelly, tell her of his revelation and explain how he felt about her—and Carlie.

He grinned, excited over the changes he intended to make in his life.

Remembering Kelly's outing with Vern, his smile dimmed. He didn't want the guy helping Carlie with her horse or giving her piggyback rides. More important, he didn't want him helping Kelly, stealing a kiss or offering her comfort. *He* wanted to do those things, and more. Much, much more.

Ben wanted to see Kelly's hair spread across his pillow like a silken flame, wearing nothing but her beautiful smile and his ring on her finger. He wanted to wake up every morning with her at his side, to share his meals, his thoughts, his burdens. Also, he wanted his huge mausoleum of a house to turn into a place of laughter and joy.

By God, he intended to make it happen.

There would be times when his profession would interfere, but he knew in his heart that Kelly could cope. If his partners had learned how to juggle their personal and professional responsibilities he could too. With Kelly as his incentive, he would.

He broke out of his reverie as the assembly clapped to welcome the first speaker. The longer he sat the more his thoughts drifted until finally he admitted the truth.

He didn't want to listen to a speaker—he wanted to be at home.

Ben glanced at his watch. If he left now he'd reach Sundance by lunchtime. Putting action to his thoughts, he strode out of the hall, took the elevator to his room on the eighth floor and began haphazardly tossing his clothes and shaving gear into his suitcase.

Twenty minutes later he approached the front desk.

'I'm checking out now. Please cancel the rest of my reservation.'

'Is everything all right, sir?' the young woman asked.

'It will be.' Ten minutes later he was speeding toward his future.

'This is the most preposterous thing I've ever read,' Vanessa stormed, throwing the five-page document onto the table as she jumped to her feet. 'Ms Evers is certainly determined to find fault with every area of this facility except her own.'

Tension charged the atmosphere in the conference room. The entire committee seemed dazed by the facts Kelly had presented in her report, but Ben's presence had done more to shatter her calm than Vanessa's outburst.

She'd been shocked when she'd seen Ben join the group moments before the meeting had convened. Had she confused the dates or had he skipped the symposium entirely? He appeared full of energy and purpose, making her wonder where he'd gone and what had happened.

As for herself, she knew what her weekend had been like. She'd written her resignation to TLC, Inc, mailing it before her courage faltered.

She'd spent hours preparing her report, and after she'd deemed it acceptable she'd begun to pack their belongings.

She'd also broken the news to her daughter. Carlie had been happy over the idea of living with Kelly instead of her grandparents, but the idea of leaving Sundance had significantly dampened her mood.

Vanessa's tirade refocused her thoughts on the situation at hand. 'Kelly Evers is nothing but a troublemaker,' she spat, glowering at her perceived nemesis.

Marvin Albertson, the hospital administrator, peered

at Vanessa over the reading glasses perched on the edge
of his hawk-like nose.

Vanessa's chilling, hate-filled gaze gave Kelly a moment's trepidation. Yet what could the woman do? Kelly
was leaving the hospital's employ in a few hours. By
tomorrow morning she wouldn't even be in town.

'Kelly isn't making any direct accusations,' Marvin
commented as he turned a page.

'Naturally, she can't,' Vanessa said smugly. 'She's
simply fabricating details to sensationalize her report so
she'll look good in your eyes.'

Ben interrupted. 'Speaking of details, Kelly lists several interesting points which warrant an explanation.
Why *are* we paying a non-existent company for supplies?'

Vanessa's mouth opened, then closed. Her eyes
glanced about furtively, as if she'd find the answer written on the walls.

Marvin addressed Hank. 'Can you shed some light on
the situation?'

Hank's face turned a sickening hue. 'Vanessa initialed
the invoices and assured me everything was in order. I
didn't have reason to believe otherwise.'

'For heaven's sake,' Vanessa snapped. 'I can prove
Global is a company because I've filed the shipping
manifests myself.'

Kelly leaned forward. 'Fine. What are we buying?'

'I can't say off the top of my head,' Vanessa said, her
voice venomous. 'I'll have to review the documents.'

'I'm glad to hear a paper trail exists,' Kelly said, 'because your staff can't find one.'

'Kelly makes a valid argument, Vanessa,' Ben interjected. 'Since this has become an issue, to satisfy our
curiosity we should see your documentation.'

Kelly's tension seemed to evaporate at the sound of

Ben's voice. His silence had seemed ominous, but he'd obviously sided with her—a comforting thought.

Vanessa rose, appearing regal in her anger. 'If you'll allow me a few minutes, I'll bring the information and put an end to this nonsense.'

Marvin nodded as he folded his arms across his chest. 'A wonderful idea. We'll wait for you.'

With a haughty sniff Vanessa glided across the room.

The purchasing agent's confidence eroded Kelly's bit by bit. For a fleeting moment she feared she might have made a terrible mistake. On the other hand, Mariah's contacts were too well established to have erred as well. She took a calming breath, clutching the pencil in her hand until her fingers ached.

Vanessa slammed the door with enough force to rattle the pictures on the wall. After the echo died Ben broke the silence.

'I'm gone for five days and everything falls apart. Can't this place run smoothly without me?' he complained good-naturedly.

The smiles on the remaining staff members' faces gradually grew wider. Everyone began to murmur at once, speculating about the outcome with the person beside him or her. Kelly felt everyone's furtive glances come her way. Those next to her discussed mundane subjects, as if the current one was taboo until Vanessa presented her own case.

Minutes ticked by. Ten, then twenty. Finally thirty.

Marvin glanced at the clock. 'Someone call Vanessa's office and find out how much longer she'll need.'

The radiology supervisor scooted his chair away from the rectangular table to obey. He returned a moment later. 'No one has seen her for the past hour.'

For a few seconds they stared at each other in horror.

Relief swept over Kelly. Vanessa's desperate actions implied guilt. Her hasty exit had convicted her.

'Call Security. If she's left the building notify the police,' Ben ordered, his gaze fixed on Kelly.

'I'll do it,' Marvin said, his voice an octave higher from the excitement. 'I hope we can keep this out of the newspaper.' He scooped the reports together, before hurrying toward his office.

Ben addressed Kelly. 'It appears we owe you a large debt.'

Kelly's face warmed. 'Just doing my job,' she said lightly, basking in his praise.

The room cleared as quickly as if a live virus had been introduced, leaving Kelly and Ben seated across from each other.

Suddenly ill at ease, Kelly gathered her pages and rose. 'I thought you'd be gone all week.'

He grinned. 'I changed my plans. I was needed here.'

'A patient?'

'No.' He didn't elaborate, but the smile on his face disappeared. 'How was your date with Vern?'

It took several seconds to marshall her thoughts. 'We didn't go. I canceled.'

'You did? Why?'

Because he wasn't you. 'Because Carlie and I were packing. Today's my last day.'

'What?' Ben looked dazed.

'The guy they hired started this morning. I could have stayed the week, but...' she shrugged '...I thought it best to leave after I turned in my report.'

Before he could ask any more questions, requiring answers she couldn't give, she changed the subject. 'How was the conference?'

He flashed a wry grin. 'I didn't attend long enough to find out. I took a detour beforehand, though. I went to see—' His pager beeped and he muttered a curse. 'Look, it's a long story and I have to go. I'll come by this evening. We'll talk then.'

'It's not a good idea—' she began.

He skirted the table, lifted her up by her elbows and planted a kiss on her mouth. 'Six-thirty. Be there.'

Kelly watched his long strides carry him out of the room, feeling once again as if someone had yanked the rug out from under her feet.

The rest of the afternoon passed by in a flurry of activity. A local policeman arrived to take Kelly's statement, advising her that other law enforcement agencies would become involved as well.

'Have you found Vanessa?' Kelly asked.

He shook his head. 'She's disappeared. We have an APB out, but she could be in two other states in a matter of minutes.'

'You think she's left town?'

'I'd bet on it. She'd be a fool to stay here. A person can't hide very well in a community where there aren't any strangers.'

She found the thought comforting. For the next hour her spirits soared over her success. However, they quickly fell to earth after she received a personal phone call.

Susannah Whipple sounded frantic. 'Carlie's missing.'

CHAPTER ELEVEN

DREAD filled every inch of Kelly's soul. 'She's what?'

'I'm so sorry,' Susannah cried. 'She asked to go to the restroom so I sent her, like I always do. When she didn't return I went looking for her. Carlie's disappeared. I feel absolutely terrible.'

Kelly struggled to think logically in spite of her worry. 'She isn't hiding on the playground?'

'No. We've searched the building and the grounds from top to bottom. Do you know where she might have gone?'

Where would she go? The question reverberated through Kelly's mind. Carlie didn't know her directions so even if she had a destination in mind she wouldn't reach it.

'Have you called the police?'

'Yes. They need her picture to show around town.'

'I'm on my way.' She flung down the receiver and grabbed her purse. 'Carlie's missing from school,' she told a stunned Dee and Lane. 'See you later.'

She ran through the door before they could reply.

Outside, the Wyoming afternoon heat shimmered on the pavement as she ran across the parking lot to her van. Squinting against the sun's brightness, she didn't notice a black BMW parked at the end of a row of cars until its powerful engine roared.

Tires squealed and the car bore down on her with Vanessa at the wheel.

Kelly's preoccupation over Carlie's whereabouts slowed her reactions. She jumped back, but her hesitation was too long. The left front fender struck her and she flew across the pavement.

The pain in her leg exceeded the pain of the street's rough surface, tearing off layers of skin. She rolled until something struck the side of her head, causing instant nausea. Darkness hovered on the edge of her vision.

Although she fought to stay alert, the pounding in her head escalated and she lost the battle.

'Ben. I need you.'

Ben glanced up from the chart in his hand to see Marlys Brenner, Sundance's physician who covered the satellite clinics, waiting at the door. He'd always seen her as cool, calm and collected, even in emergencies, but now he sensed an uncharacteristic agitation in her. Something must be serious for her to pull him away from his own emergency.

'Excuse me,' he told his patient, a sixty-year-old man, complaining of chest pain, before he handed the chart with his orders to the waiting nurse.

As soon as he stepped into the hallway Marlys grabbed his arm and propelled him forward. 'An ambulance just brought Kelly into ER. Someone ran over her in the parking lot.'

Instant fear gripped his heart and he lengthened his steps to reach the ER. 'How bad?' he asked.

Marlys matched his pace, almost running to do so. 'Jim and Allen are assessing her now. Last I heard her collar-bone is broken. Her left leg, too, in at least three places.'

'Internal injuries?'

'We're not sure yet. Vern started taking the films just before I came to get you.'

'Did she get a good look at the driver?' he asked, rounding the final corner.

Marlys stopped outside the swing doors leading to Emergency. 'We don't know. She was unconscious when the ER staff got to her. She regained consciousness on the way inside, but she's extremely agitated.'

'Head trauma?'

Marlys shrugged. 'Preliminary exam doesn't indicate more than the bump on her head, but she's not making sense. Maybe you can calm her. The police want to talk to her as soon as possible.'

He ran his hands through his hair. 'When did it happen?'

'Ten, fifteen minutes ago. An office girl saw a black car leaving the scene,' Marlys continued, 'but she wasn't close enough to see the license plate. The cops are fairly sure Vanessa's responsible.'

He squared his jaw in frustration. Then, impatient to see Kelly, he placed his palm on the door to push it aside.

Marlys stepped in front of him, blocking his entrance. 'I know you're upset. You're also too close to the situation to make sound medical decisions. From what I've heard, you're the nearest thing she has to family.'

'Damn right.'

'So let Jim and Allen do their thing while I take care of your patient. You act as an objective bystander. OK?'

He hesitated, then nodded.

Entering the trauma room a minute later, his gut tightened at the sight of a blood-spattered Kelly on the gurney, her neck, arm and shoulder immobilized. Her cries of distress bothered him most of all.

He loved her so. He couldn't bear to think of how he'd manage if she didn't recover. Without sophisticated imagery techniques, he could only guess what was happening inside her head. He tried to remain positive, channeling his thoughts away from the worst-case scenario.

For the moment it was all he could do.

Kelly's body felt as if it was on fire. The staff weren't helping matters either as they pulled, tugged, inserted needles and flashed lights in her eyes. However, none of her physical pain compared to the utter despair in her heart.

She couldn't explain why she felt the way she did. Her thoughts were disjointed and her head ached in time to her heartbeat.

Suddenly Ben hovered over her, enfolding her free hand in his. 'Just relax,' he said in a soothing voice. 'You're going to be fine.'

A measure of relief spread through her. She was so glad to see him. Surely she could make him believe that something bigger than the accident was upsetting her. 'Please... You must...' she mumbled.

'Her neuro signs are good, but her mental state is lousy,' Jim said, from his place near her feet. 'She hasn't been coherent and keeps fighting us. If she continues we'll have to restrain her.'

Restrain her? Kelly tried to rise. She had to leave. She had something important to do. If only her scrambled brain would sort her thoughts properly.

'Need...to leave. Something's...wrong.'

Ben leaned over her, pinning her onto the gurney. 'Relax. Everything's fine.'

'The circulation in her foot is poor,' Jim reported, speaking as if Kelly couldn't hear. 'She needs a vascular surgeon, along with an orthopedic man. They'll probably run a CT scan of her head too. I've already notified the life flight. The helicopter is on its way.'

They wanted to send her away? They couldn't! 'No!' Kelly sobbed. 'I...can't... Don't send...me.'

Ben didn't release his firm hold and she felt trapped. 'There's nothing to be afraid of. I'll go along. You have to calm down.'

Frustrated tears streamed down her face. 'Something's wrong...' Her voice faded.

'What's wrong?' he asked.

'I don't know. Don't remember. But something's wrong,' she insisted.

'Carlie will be fine. I'll look after her myself.' He brushed away the stray locks of hair from her forehead.

Carlie. Kelly's fear and the feeling of helplessness escalated. Again her frustration over her inability to marshall her thoughts built to massive proportions. 'When you said her name...something with Carlie.'

She stilled, closing her eyes to concentrate. She remembered a meeting, Vanessa's anger. Her mind skipped to a picture of Vanessa, bearing down on her. She shuddered.

'Where does it hurt?' Ben asked. The concern in his voice changed to a demanding tone as he addressed his cohorts. 'Can't you give her something for pain?'

She ignored him, unwilling to take the time to catalog her aches when her mind was starting to function. Something had happened before she'd seen Vanessa in the parking lot.

She'd received a phone call. It had been from... Her eyes shot open. The fog in her head receded to the outer edges. 'Carlie's gone,' she cried, trying to rise. 'I have to find her.'

Ben's face blanched. 'She's missing? Are you sure?'

'Yes.' Her voice was husky. If anything happened to her daughter... If she never saw her again... Never again hugged her tiny body, answered her million and one questions, felt her sweet, sloppy kisses or wiped away her tears... Kelly would die.

A lump formed in her throat and her chest burned with an emotional pain far greater than the physical pain in her body. She couldn't lose Carlie. She couldn't!

The entire staff standing around her froze in disbelief. 'It's true,' she insisted, afraid they would dismiss her claim as delusional due to head trauma.

'I'll check it out.' Cheryl left the gathering and returned a few minutes later, her face pale.

'Kelly's right,' she reported, obviously flabbergasted by what she'd learned. 'Dee said the day-care center called earlier. Her daughter wandered away around two o'clock this afternoon.'

'Please. I have to find her.' Kelly's sentences grew longer, her pronunciation less slurred. 'Let me go...so I can look.'

'You aren't in any shape to do anything but lie here,' Ben said sternly. 'Don't worry. I'll find her. She couldn't have gone far.'

'The police are at the center. They need...her photo,' Kelly said. 'In my billfold.'

Ben glanced around the room. 'Where's her purse?'

Someone thrust it at him. He sifted through the bag, retrieving the snapshot out of the wallet. 'I'll take it over right away,' he said.

Kelly closed her eyes. 'Thanks.' She reached for his hand and squeezed. 'Find her for me.'

He kissed her cheek. 'I will. I promise.'

'She's all I have,' Kelly choked out.

'You have me,' he said softly. 'I love her too, and I *will* find her.'

The steady 'thwop' of helicopter rotors grew louder. 'Chopper's here,' Jim commented.

Kelly's eyes flew open. 'I won't go yet. I have to be

here. What if she's hurt...and needs me?' She groaned, imagining the worst.

'You need a specialist,' Ben said. 'The circulation below your knee is impaired. It has to be restored before the damage is irreparable. I'm sure Carlie's hiding somewhere, having the time of her life.'

Her eyes glistened with tears and her mouth quivered. 'She wouldn't do that. I don't care about my foot. Please don't make me leave. Not yet.'

'How will you race after her with one leg?' he asked, sounding brutally practical. 'I'll bring Carlie to you. By then you won't scare her with all this apparatus.'

She bit her lip. His logic was compelling, but her motherly protectiveness wouldn't let go.

'You can count on me. I won't let you down,' he said.

Kelly stared into his eyes. Determination shone out of the depths and purpose squared his jaw. Ben was a man of his word; she knew it in her heart.

Her sigh caught in her throat. Finally she nodded, accepting the inevitable.

'Just relax. Concentrate on getting better and I'll do the rest.'

Reassured by his promise, the stress of the day began to overwhelm her. She felt herself drifting. 'My hero,' she mumbled.

Ben watched the tension leave Kelly's body as the pain medication began to work. Her faith in him was humbling and he hoped to deserve the status she'd awarded him.

'Call me if her condition changes,' he ordered on his way out. He drove straight to the day-care center, spoke with Susannah Whipple and Al Tompkins, the officer assigned to the case, and explained his thoughts about a kidnapping.

Al conferred with his colleagues by radio. 'It's pos-

sible, but doubtful,' he reported to Susannah and Ben.
'The child disappeared a little before Ms Osbourne did.
But we won't know for sure until we find either one or
both of them.'

Ben took comfort in Al's opinion, but, he knew total
peace wouldn't come until Carlie was safe in his care.

Al left with the photo to make copies for distribution
and Ben began to cruise the streets. Where would she
go? Why had she left? Suddenly he had an idea.

Percy would find her.

He turned in the opposite direction and stepped on the
accelerator. Minutes later, with Percy beside him, he
backtracked to the day-care center and parked in front
of the building.

'Find Carlie,' he instructed the Dalmatian. 'Look for
Carlie.'

Percy wandered around the yard, sniffing as he went.
Before long he bounded away.

Ben followed, hoping the animal wasn't on the trail
of a cat. He didn't intend to fail in his task. He wouldn't
rest until he found Carlie.

The medical helicopter flew overhead on its way east
to Rapid City. Knowing Kelly was counting on him he
urged Percy on.

The Dalmatian led him to the park, the one where
Deke and Troy had had their altercation weeks earlier.
Had Carlie come this far, crossing several busy streets
to do so?

With a vindictive Vanessa on the loose—a woman
who had no qualms about attempting murder—he could
only pray that the police were right and that she wasn't
responsible for Carlie's disappearance.

Thoughts of failure spurred him to watch for any signs
that indicated Carlie had traveled this path.

Percy raced to the imagination station, sniffing his

way around until he stopped underneath an enclosed lookout section. He barked.

'Is she up there?' Ben asked the dog.

Percy woofed again.

A familiar strawberry-blonde head poked through the porthole-sized opening. 'Percy? Dr Ben?'

Ben closed his eyes and sent up a silent prayer of thanks. What a welcome sight! 'We're here, Carlie. Come on down.'

Carlie crawled through the intricate maze of hollow tubes and slid down the chute to land in his waiting arms.

He hugged her close. 'Everyone was so worried about you.'

'Mommy said we were leaving tomorrow. I wanted to go to your house and tell Percy goodbye.' She wiped at the dried trail of tears on her dirty face. 'But I got lost.'

Ben stroked her hair. 'Percy deserves a special treat for finding you, don't you think?'

She nodded. 'Is Mommy upset? Where is she?'

He lifted her in his arms. 'Your mom had an accident. She's going to be fine, though,' he said, as her eyes brimmed with fresh tears. 'Did you see the helicopter that flew over a little bit ago?'

Her head bobbed up and down.

'Your mother was in that helicopter. She's on her way to a big hospital where they can fix her up better than we can here. I promised to bring you to see her just as soon as possible.'

'She couldn't wait for me?'

'No, half-pint. She wanted to, but she had to go.' At Carlie's crestfallen expression, he added, 'We'll be there in about an hour. That's not too long to wait, is it?'

She screwed up her face. 'S'pose not.'

'Come on. There are a lot of people looking for you, and I need to tell them you're safe and sound.'

He forced her chin up so she could meet his gaze. 'Don't ever do something like this again,' he scolded.

'I won't,' she said, laying her head on his shoulder.

Ben hugged her again. 'Good. Let's go home.'

As soon as he'd called off the search Ben notified the hospital and asked them to pass the word along to Kelly. After packing a bag for himself and Carlie, he headed for Rapid City.

Nearly a week passed by and Kelly felt crabby. With her leg in a cast and her right arm immobilized, the surgeon had rendered her virtually helpless. The scrapes on her body had scabbed over and were starting to itch, but she couldn't reach most of them—a frustrating situation if Ben's hands weren't available.

She was tired of spending only a few minutes a day with Carlie, relying on reports from friends and visitors about her well-being. She'd relived the bone-chilling fear too many times upon awakening in this hospital bed. If not for Ben's nearly constant presence and reassurances that the nightmare of Carlie's disappearance had ended, she didn't know how she would have coped.

All in all, she was tired of being a patient. 'I want to go home,' she told Ben without preamble as he walked through the doorway of her private room.

He laughed before he kissed her. 'I can tell which dwarf you are today. Grumpy. Maybe my news will cheer you up. Vanessa is in custody.'

'What a relief,' Kelly said, her spirits brightening. 'I was afraid I'd have to look over my shoulder for the rest of my life.' She shuddered, remembering the car bearing down on her and the moment of impact.

'How's the leg?' he asked.

She welcomed the change of subject. 'Great. When can I go home?'

'As soon as you agree to marry me,' he said solemnly.

She blinked and shook her head. Obviously she'd heard wrong. 'What did you say?'

'I'm asking you to marry me.'

Her pulse rate accelerated. 'Rather a drastic measure in order to be discharged, wouldn't you say?'

He shrugged. 'That's the condition.'

She studied his face, trying to read his expression. 'What about Tanya and Alyce and your patients and wanting an independent wife—'

'Seeing you in ER took ten years off my life. I lost a few more when Carlie disappeared. I want a future.' He gripped her hand. 'As for an independent wife, I found her. Even though she can expose criminal activity and leap tall buildings in a single bound...' he grinned '...I want the right to be called whenever she or her daughter need something.'

Kelly closed her eyes, her throat choked with emotion. 'I've waited so long to hear you say that,' she whispered. 'Carlie will be thrilled.'

'She is.'

'You've already told her?'

Ben nodded. 'It was the only way she'd go home with your parents. I promised that as soon as you were well enough to leave the hospital I'd bring her back to Sundance.'

She paused. 'Are you sure? About marriage, that is. It's a big step, you know. We don't have to rush into it. We can wait—'

'Until you're on your feet in a few weeks,' he interjected. 'And, yes, I'm sure. I've never been more certain of anything in my entire life. I love you. I want to be

Carlie's father and a father to all the other children you want to have.'

'I love you too. I accept your proposal. For better or for worse.' Her eyes brimmed with tears of happiness. Holding out for her hero had finally paid off.

It was Mother's Day, eighteen months later.

'We have a favor to ask you, Tom.'

Seated on the sofa to work on her art assignment, Kelly watched Ben as he spoke into the receiver. They'd left a message on Tom's answering machine several hours earlier and he'd finally returned their call.

'Put him on the speaker,' Kelly instructed.

Ben complied. As he sank next to her she heard her brother-in-law's voice come through loud and clear. 'Tell Kelly happy Mother's Day.'

'Thanks,' she called out.

'So, what's the big favor?' Tom asked. 'If it's baby-sitting, you know I'd be happy to watch Carlie. Although why you need someone to look after her with Percy around is beyond me.'

Kelly glanced at Ben and chuckled. Her heart swelled with love as she gazed at her husband. Giving in to her feelings, she placed the artist's pad on the coffee-table, next to the mug of hot tea and the bowl of crackers. Then, tucking her good leg underneath her, she rose to snake her arms around his neck and nuzzle his ear.

Ben slipped an arm around her waist. 'Sorry. That's not why we phoned,' he said.

'Hurry up and ask him,' she whispered, tracing a line along the side of his face.

'I'm trying,' Ben said, appearing both amused and exasperated.

'You're trying what?' Tom responded.

'Never mind. I was talking to Kelly.' Ben cleared his

throat. 'We're calling because you're going to be an uncle and we want you to be the godfather.'

'No kidding. That's great! I'm happy for you guys. And, yes, I'd be honored to be the man of the hour.'

'Thanks,' Kelly responded.

'How's the studying?' Ben asked.

'Intense. I'm going to take a long vacation when my exams are over. Find a beach, sip margaritas and let the sand run between my toes.'

'Surrounded by beautiful women, no doubt.'

'Just one. A tall, leggy blonde. No offense, Kelly.'

'None taken,' she said. Tom had always teased her about her height and often reminded Carlie to eat her vegetables so she wouldn't stunt her growth and end up being short like her mother.

'Wearing something exotic, I'm sure,' Ben said dryly, exchanging a smile with Kelly. Suddenly his gaze turned hungry, as if he wanted to devour her inch by inch.

Moved by Ben's appreciation and ignoring her brother-in-law's reply, Kelly unbuttoned the top fastening of her flannel shirt.

Ben's eyes lit up like candles on a birthday cake. Without a second invitation he took care of the next three. He stroked her womanly curves through the satin camisole, bringing her body to a feverish awareness that begged for fulfillment. She closed her eyes and purred like a kitten as she rubbed her knee against him.

He jumped off the sofa and rushed to the phone. 'Can't talk now,' he said crisply. 'Kelly needs me.' He broke the connection in the middle of Tom's guffaw.

'It's about time you told him goodbye,' Kelly murmured, joining him in the center of the room. 'Carlie will be coming home from Mary Lou's house in about an hour and we still need to load the car for our picnic.

Since my stomach isn't on the warpath, I don't want to waste a minute of this Mother's Day.'

This particular holiday would always hold a special place in her heart. For the first time in her life she could celebrate motherhood with a loving husband at her side.

'Don't worry, we won't,' he said. Starting at her mouth, he kissed his way down to her breasts.

Kelly sighed audibly. The next instant Ben lifted her off the floor and strode toward the staircase.

'I can walk.' Physical therapy had done its job—she walked with only a slight limp and that was only after she'd overtaxed herself.

'I know. This is faster.' He winked.

In short order their clothing lay in an untidy heap on the master bedroom floor. Ben sighed with delight and masculine appreciation shone out of his eyes.

Suddenly shy, Kelly placed her palm on the curve of her abdomen where his child resided.

Moving her hand to kiss the slight swell, he whispered, 'You're beautiful.' Seconds later he swept her onto the queen-sized bed, careful not to crush her under his weight as he brought her ecstasy and his own release.

Later, as they lay entwined under the comforter and satiated by their love-making, he spoke. 'Carlie wants to buy the Dalmatian advertised in the newspaper.'

'Mmm,' she answered, reveling in the feel of her naked body against his.

'She told me that as she's going to have a playmate Percy needs one too. She's already chosen a name.' He grinned. 'Prudence.'

'I suppose you're going to be a soft touch and give her what she wants,' she chided without heat.

'Was there any doubt?'

Kelly grinned. 'I know she's only six, but you're making it difficult for her to have any future boyfriends.'

'Why do you say that?' he asked.

'None of them will measure up to you. I overheard her talking to Mary Lou the other day as they were playing house. She announced that she wants a hero like her mommy has.'

Ben rose on one elbow, his grin wide. The two women in his life had treated him like a superstar ever since he'd found Carlie at the park. 'Really? She actually said that?'

She nodded. 'I plan to remind her of it when she gets older. I don't want her ever to settle for second-best. The right man is well worth the wait.'

'I'm glad you think so,' he murmured, stroking the curve of her hip as he reveled in his good fortune. The past year had brought a lot of changes to his life, and by the next Mother's Day there would be more.

He could hardly wait.

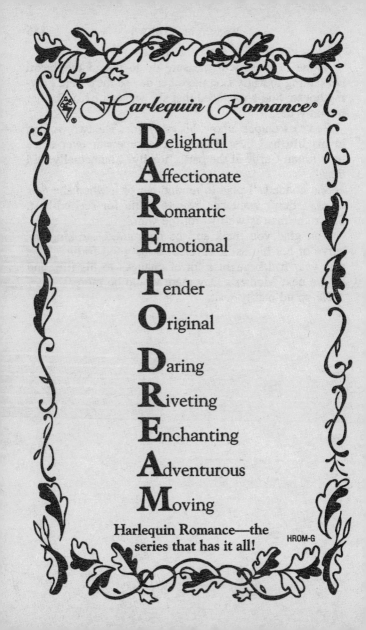

Harlequin Romance®

Delightful

Affectionate

Romantic

Emotional

Tender

Original

Daring

Riveting

Enchanting

Adventurous

Moving

Harlequin Romance—the
series that has it all!

HROM-G

HARLEQUIN PRESENTS®

HARLEQUIN PRESENTS
men you won't be able to resist
falling in love with...

HARLEQUIN PRESENTS
women who have feelings
just like your own...

HARLEQUIN PRESENTS
powerful passion in
exotic international settings...

HARLEQUIN PRESENTS
intense, dramatic stories that will keep you
turning to the very last page...

HARLEQUIN PRESENTS
The world's bestselling romance series!

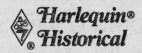

Harlequin® Historical

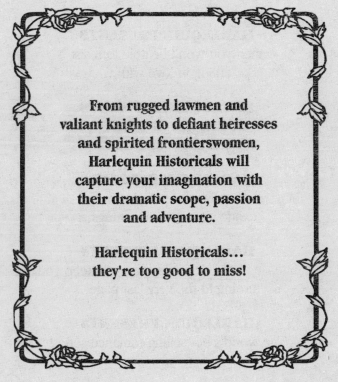

From rugged lawmen and
valiant knights to defiant heiresses
and spirited frontierswomen,
Harlequin Historicals will
capture your imagination with
their dramatic scope, passion
and adventure.

Harlequin Historicals...
they're too good to miss!

LOOK FOR OUR FOUR FABULOUS MEN!

Each month some of today's bestselling authors bring four new fabulous men to Harlequin American Romance. Whether they're rebel ranchers, millionaire power brokers or sexy single dads, they're all gallant princes—and they're all ready to sweep you into lighthearted fantasies and contemporary fairy tales where anything is possible and where all your dreams come true!

You don't even have to make a wish…
Harlequin American Romance will grant your every desire!

Look for Harlequin American Romance
wherever Harlequin books are sold!

HARLEQUIN SUPERROMANCE®

...there's more to the story!

Superromance. A *big* satisfying read about unforget-
table characters. Each month we offer
four very different stories that range from family
drama to adventure and mystery, from highly emotional stories to romantic comedies—and
much more! Stories about people you'll
believe in and care about. Stories too
compelling to put down....

Our authors are among today's *best* romance writ-
ers. You'll find familiar names and
talented newcomers. Many of them are
award winners—and you'll see why!

If you want the biggest and best
in romance fiction, you'll get it
from Superromance!

Available wherever Harlequin books are sold.